THIS WILL HURT

PART I OF II

CARA DEE

This Will Hurt I
Copyright © 2023 by Cara Dee
All rights reserved

Edited by Silently Correcting Your Grammar, LLC.
Formatted by Eliza Rae Services.

PROLOGUE
2010

Jake Denver

Something told me I was gonna remember this guy for a long time to come.

I grinned as he completely missed his mark, and I had to shift the camera to follow his passionate rambling about an old bird. The California condor. I'd thought he'd worn his "Save the Sea Otters" tee as some ironic joke, but I was beginning to wonder if there was an activist in Roe Finlay.

Standing somewhere in the middle of Big Sur's state park, surrounded by redwoods and bright-green shrubs, I captured every moment of his unscripted speech. Because that was our deal. No script. We'd see what we'd see, and he would talk about it.

I signaled to him to stay put below one of the tall trees, so I could leave the camera on its tripod and grab my other one for some stills.

"Okay, we'll totally edit this part out," he said, "but I sort of see us as condors."

I chuckled silently, watching him through the lens. "We're scavenging vultures?"

"Well, kind of!" he laughed. "Not just us, but LA people—especially those tryna make it in the business. We'll take whatever we can get our hands on."

I could see his point. And I could capture his lazy, dimpled grin as he scratched the side of his head and peered up at the hole in the tree. That was where he insisted a condor had laid an egg. He'd said it fit their behavior. Condors didn't build their own nests; they used what was out there.

"It's about more than scavenging, though," he continued thoughtfully. "Condors are survivors—with a little bit of help. Kinda like you and me. We get by, but not on our own. We have help too. Just like the condors around here had some thirty years ago when they were almost extinct."

I glanced up from my camera and listened to him.

He smirked after a moment of silence. "We may not have a ten-foot wingspan, but we're scrappy, aren't we?"

I smiled. "I guess so. But I won't eat roadkill."

He laughed.

I didn't know if he was right in his comparison, but I did know that without his storming into my life, I wouldn't be visiting Big Sur for the first time today, and I sure as fuck wouldn't be filming a pilot for a travel show that so far only existed in our very new dream.

"Let's see if we can find a banana slug," Roe suggested.

Another thing I definitely wouldn't be doing today if it weren't for him.

Hunting slugs.

CHAPTER 1
2010

*J*ust *go home, you fucking moron. You don't belong in LA.*

I made my way across campus, feeling more out of place every time I left class. Me? Taking a videography class? Christ on a fucking... My pop was right. I should go back home and join the family business. I was too old to be entering a field I knew nothing about.

Almost nothing.

I was leaving behind a good career in the Marines for... random classes at Santa Monica College. Learn videography in twelve weeks. Study the art of documentary filmmaking in one semester. Then I thought about why I'd left the service. How sick I was of seeing death through my lens. Combat photography had been such a fucking fluke anyway. I was infantry. I was more at home on the front lines in Afghanistan than... But no. No. No, I was here because I couldn't stand the war anymore. I didn't wanna see another dead soldier, hear another explosion, witness another crying child surrounded by blood and debris.

I went to the coffee shop on the corner of the street where Nikki worked. She had the car, and we'd go home together once she was off her shift.

I ordered a coffee and found an empty table by one of the windows.

Sounded pretty good, though, didn't it? Go home with my girlfriend at the end of the day... Except, it was her car, her apartment, and my savings were almost gone. By next month, I'd have to take that bartending job in West Hollywood where the tips were so good.

By then, I'd be twenty-seven. March was right around the corner.

Option one. The Marines. Go back as a full-time war photographer and see all the suffering up close once more. Option two, head home to Norfolk and spend the rest of my days working alongside my old man.

With a heavy sigh, I flattened my notebook against the table, and I heard Nikki in the back of my head, telling me again to buy a damn backpack or something. I kept rolling up my notebook when I had nothing else to fidget with—but I wasn't buying a bag for a single textbook and notebook.

I retrieved my pen from the inner pocket of my jacket, and I opened the notebook.

Final project. Final project, final project, final project. I needed *content*. I understood filming. Documenting. But coming up with my own content for a fucking college class's final project? I was doomed.

"There you are! Fuck, I thought I lost you, man."

I furrowed my brow and glanced toward the man's voice—that belonged to someone I definitely didn't know. But he was coming toward my table, and he was staring right at me.

No, wait. I recognized him. He was in my class, wasn't he? Out here, I had developed a radar for East Coast people, and he had a New York accent. Otherwise, not much about him stood out. Average height, brown hair like mine, fairly fit, on the lanky side, probably a bit younger than me.

He sat down in front of me, out of breath, and removed his messenger bag. "Look, I'm just gonna come out and say it. I have two hundred bucks, I'm living in my truck, and I have *one* network connection that I desperately wanna use. He told me to send him my final project—see if he could make some calls—but as has become painfully clear in this class, videography isn't my thing. I understand fuck-all about goddamn HDV, SxS, and the difference between standard definition and hi-def." He leaned forward. "Dude, y'all were talking about memory cards, and I thought we were discussing a fucking festival in Austin."

That...was SXSW. South by Southwest.

"Anyway—in short, I have an idea," he went on. "It has an artistic approach, but I'll admit, it's more of a come-hither for networks, something I think will sell. To get a foot in the door. But I need a partner, and I've watched you in class. You know your way around the equipment and the editing software. When the professor asks his dumb, insane questions, you actually know the answers."

Was this how he talked to people he'd never met before? I didn't even know his name.

I guessed if you were desperate enough and living out of your car, you cut to the chase faster.

That might very well be me in the near future.

So if he had an idea...

I extended my hand. "I'm Jake."

He gave me a puzzled look, before he seemed to remember he'd just jumped into the conversation with no preamble. Then he flashed a dimpled grin and shook my hand.

"Roe. It's Monroe, but everyone calls me Roe."

Roe, then.

That weekend, I got up at the ass-crack of dawn and carried my most valuable possessions down the stairs from Nikki's apartment to the curb where Roe waited in his beat-up truck.

"Mornin', Jake."

"Hey, man."

The back seat was littered with proof of his actually living in his truck. He smiled apologetically and was quick to push his backpack, some clothes, a pillow, a sleeping bag, and a couple plastic bags to the left side. I felt my forehead crease, but I said nothing and sat my hardcase next to my duffels. Two cameras, grip, tripod, separate audio recorder, mic... I was confident I had everything we needed for our project.

And safe to say, we had a lot riding on this. Roe needed an actual address, and I wouldn't mind not living off my girlfriend. At this point, I could swing about a third of the rent, most of our food, utilities, and gas.

"Jake!"

I turned my ball cap backward and looked up toward the apartment, only to see Nikki running down the stairs, wearing nothing but a pair of skimpy shorts and one of my tees. Okay, it was fine—I didn't mind her wearing my clothes, but when she twisted the bottom into a knot, she stretched the fabric.

"Damn," Roe muttered.

I threw him a smirk. "Eyes to yourself, buddy."

He chuckled and ran a hand through his hair.

I faced Nikki again, and she flashed a cute, sleepy grin and held up a paper bag.

"You forgot your sandwiches, babe."

Oh, right. Shit.

"Thanks. What would I do without you?" I smiled and shook my head. She just squeezed my hand and eyed Roe, so I figured introductions were in order. "Nikki, the guy who's gonna make us rich. Roe, my girlfriend—future stylist to the stars."

"Oh, I hope all that will come true," Nikki laughed. "Good to meet you, Roe."

"You too." Roe smiled and offered a two-finger salute from the other side of the truck. "I'll have your man back tomorrow at the latest."

"Sounds good to me." She beamed and reached up to me, and I gave her a kiss. "Have a fun trip. I'm gonna get ready for work."

"Text me when you get home," I requested. We didn't live in the safest neighborhood, and I didn't like her being out on her own at night. The walk from the parking lot was enough for me to usually meet up with her.

"I promise." She gave my hand another squeeze, and then she backed off as I got in the truck.

Seconds later, Roe pulled away from the curb, and we started our journey toward Big Sur.

If we ever got there. Roe might kill us. He drove...recklessly. Thank fuck the streets weren't too crowded at this hour on a Saturday.

I cleared my throat and buckled my seat belt.

"You been together long?" he asked.

Uh. I scratched my chin. "'Bout four months, I guess. Or five, if you count the month before we were broken up for like a week."

Nikki was...awesome in one way and less so in another. Woman had a temper, and I was pretty mellow. Too mellow, in her opinion. She thought I didn't give a fuck because I didn't get heated like her.

When we'd met, she'd flirted her sweet ass off, calling me everything from a bad boy to someone who had to be a "quarterback or something." Which I'd heard before. I got it. I had the looks of someone who could be an arrogant asshole. I'd attracted the popular girls all my life, but they grew bored with me fast.

I had no doubt Nikki would do that too. Sooner or later.

"I had an on-and-off thing with my high-school girlfriend. Both addictive and destructive."

Roe wasn't completely wrong. Addictive was a strong word, but there was certainly never a dull moment around Nikki. In the time we'd been dating, I'd been to more nightclubs than I cared to remember. She was always...*on.*

"I'm along for the ride till she finds someone more exciting," I said. "What about you? Are you seeing anyone?" I grabbed the handle above me as he swerved between cars to make our turn for the on-ramp to the 405. "Maybe you could find a cute driving instructor."

"You sound like my brothers and sister," he chuckled. "Dating will have to wait. I can't afford distractions right now."

I knew the feeling. At the same time, I'd rather stay with Nikki than in the two-bedroom I'd crashed at before. With six other dudes who were hoping to make it big in Los Angeles. I could not get out of that rat-infested testosterone soup fast enough.

"Have you been in town long?" I wondered.

"What—I don't sound like a local?"

I grinned.

He shook his head in amusement. "Almost a year. Had a

sweet little studio when I came out here too—rented from a friend who got a job in Tokyo. But when I ran out of money, I helped him find a more reliable tenant. You?"

I released the handlebar again. Weirdly, he drove more carefully on the highway.

"About the same," I replied. "It's been eight months of being five minutes away from buying a ticket back to Norfolk."

He snorted. "Tell me about it. Then I think about what's waiting for me back home, and I'm like, I don't fucking think so. Half my family's in the Middle East, another part is poppin' out kids, and the last bunch is just tryna make ends meet."

I nodded slowly and removed my ball cap, tossing it onto the dash in front of me.

Many of us had loved ones in the Middle East.

I had a couple cousins there myself, and I'd recently spent six years going back and forth, reupping as soon as I'd been allowed. We had an entire generation feeding on hatred and vengeance.

That was why I'd started picking up my camera on my days off. To document the reality of war, of what we'd gone through, of what we saw over there on a daily basis, and what that did to us. Because eventually, we rotated back home—if we were lucky —and our family members weren't prepared.

"You're former military, aren't you?" Roe asked. "You learn the signs after a while. How you stand and walk a little differently. Always alert..."

I nodded with a dip of my chin. "I was in the Marines."

"Figures," he sighed. "I have several brothers in that branch. Thankfully, they're getting out soon. Our family's lost enough."

Ah. Yeah, that had definitely been a surefire way to recruit troops—and the way he'd phrased that, plus with his being from New York, it was all too easy to assume they'd lost someone when the towers came down. Maybe more than one.

"I actually wanted to enlist too, but everyone blew up on me," he chuckled. "Before I knew it, I was getting calls from Afghanistan. 'Whaddaya fuckin' nuts? You gonna get yourself killed ova' hea'!'" He shook his head, and I couldn't help but share his smile. Those protective family members were nice to have. "I'm the baby in the family," he explained. "I couldn't catch a damn break before 9/11 either. But everything obviously got worse after..."

I watched his expression grow more somber. Maybe he got lost in a memory. I'd learned he was twenty-four now, so he'd just been a kid when the towers came down almost a decade ago.

I phrased myself as carefully as I could. "Can I ask who you lost?"

"My parents and an uncle." He nodded once. Jesus. Both his mom and dad. "Ma worked at a bank, and my pop and uncle were firefighters. I'd like to think Pop found her—that they died together."

Fucking hell. I averted my gaze out the window. I'd heard so many similar stories over the years, but I still felt the same hatred simmering below the surface. I'd just gotten better at handling it.

"As a Marine yourself," he said, "how do you reconcile needing justice and not wanting to see innocent people get hurt?"

That was the million-dollar question, wasn't it?

"You don't." Unfortunately. "The problem is, at first, when your own hurt is fresh, you don't see innocent people at all. It's an age-old tactic used to protect the troops, to keep them from hesitatin'—you dehumanize and demonize the enemy, basically turning every face you see over there into a terrorist hijacker. Classic war propaganda. We're the good, they're the evil."

He nodded pensively. "And so we keep the war machine running."

Night and day.

I'd seen too much suffering on our side to be objective, but I was no longer under any illusions either. The first time I'd had a photo published, I'd been sick with conflict and doubt. We'd been outside Fallujah, and I'd taken a picture of an American soldier carrying a listless child with blood all over his face and legs. Questions had started piling up within me. Was this what we were fighting for? When was it gonna be enough? At what point did we decide that enough innocent lives had been lost? Was there even a way to win? The cost was already steeper than most could comprehend.

I didn't wanna think about it anymore. I would always remember the first friend who died next to me, the first time I saw an IED go off under a Humvee, the time I got shot in my shoulder, that feeling when Ma had sent a care package, letters from my baby sister, the too-familiar sound of cleaning your rifle, the smell of...

No. I was done. I would always remember, and that was enough.

I'd come to LA to learn how to see beauty instead. My distant dream was to become a documentary filmmaker. I wanted to travel the world and see things that didn't make me wanna kill myself. I wanted to convince myself that humankind could create remarkable things too.

Hell, humankind didn't even need to be involved. I wanted to see nature and animals. Something deep inside me yearned for simplicity and the untouched. Our little trip to Big Sur was a great start. I'd never been up there before.

I liked Roe's idea too. A fuckload, to be honest. He wanted to shoot our video like a pilot, because he literally hoped his "network connection" might want more. All our eggs went into this basket.

The $100 Vagabonds was the working title. We'd each pitched in fifty bucks, which would cover the whole twenty-four-hour trip for two people. Gas, food, an overnight stay.

The one thing I wasn't entirely comfortable with yet was his hope to put me in front of the camera, as some sort of cohost. I was supposed to be on the other side of the lens, but he'd given me a whole harangue about adding comedy and reeling in viewers. We had to make it interesting for those who didn't care about Big Sur, he'd said.

I groaned as I stretched, feeling every goddamn part of me pop. Jesus Christ. I loved a good road trip, but a seven-hour ride required more than two stops. Unfortunately, we were on the clock here with a lot to do in little time.

It was fucking stunning up here, though. And the air was so fresh.

I took a deep breath and looked out over the impressive cliffs and rock formations. The ocean was the deepest blue shade, the cliffs dark and sharp, and we were surrounded by greenery that was actually green and not yellow.

We'd pulled over at a rest stop that had seen better days. It was just a patch of gravel with enough space for two cars and a couple picnic tables. We hoped the run-down feel of it would keep tourists away, because the other stops we'd passed had been packed with people. The sun was shining, barely any clouds in the sky, and it wasn't too chilly.

While Roe prepared for our late lunch shoot at one of the tables, I got my camera set up near the end, so we'd both fit in the frame. The lighting was good if we kept the state park in the background as opposed to the ocean. The massive trees blocked some of the sunlight.

I attached my camera on a mount before involving the tripod. It would allow me to turn the camera without any jostling. Roe wanted to give our fictional audience a good view after our intro talk, and I had my own idea for how we could handle that transition.

He'd spent the last two hours on the road giving me a glimpse into his mind, and I had to admit I was liking his idea more and more. With the economy the way it was, it felt like a good show at the right time. Budget travel, just two buddies exploring our country, a bit of comedy, no cutting out the bloopers—not just showing the majestic scenery but the treks in between the tourist spots too.

Roe didn't want much of a script, and I liked that. We had a list of things to mention, talking points, but we'd try to get there naturally.

I bent over the camera to check the shot, making sure we'd both be in it, and I asked Roe to take a seat so I could make final adjustments.

"What's that handle thing on the side for?" he asked.

I spoke while watching him through the lens. "So I can turn the camera toward the ocean easier. I was thinking—you'll say something like, so here we are, we wanna show you Big Sur, our backyard or whatever it was you said, and then I will turn the camera and show them the view."

"Oh, I like that. That sounds cool."

We'd see how the theory transferred to reality. I might have to morph two shots if the lighting became too bright and we lost focus, but it shouldn't be a problem. The more I learned about the editing process, the easier it was to see possibilities. The sound of cars driving by would be edited out later, the cacophony of the sea gulls might fade into the background a bit more, and simple things like throat-clearing and coughing and a misplaced chuckle could be eliminated too.

Okay, last check. Everything looked good, and I'd raised the camera enough so that the road wouldn't be in the shot when I turned it around later.

"I think we're good to go—"

"Before we begin—before you push record," he said quickly. "I wanna discuss something."

"Yeah?" I sat down across from him and grabbed my sandwich bag. We'd stopped for Denny's on the way, saving our packed lunch for now when we couldn't show off any known brands and whatever.

"Two things, actually," he amended. "First thing—when we get to this part of the pilot, the viewer has already gotten the gist of the show. Like, we're doing budget traveling, the rule is we only get to spend a hundred bucks, and so on and so on. And I will make a pitch to John about our idea to use flyover footage—you will look into what it would cost to rent a drone..."

I nodded him along. That was on my list.

"So here's the second thing," he went on. "I know how to talk. I know how to sell an idea I believe in—but I still wanna show John as much as possible. Which is why I think we should do a second episode too."

I frowned, confused.

He launched into an explanation while he emptied our Cokes into two plastic cups. "In short, this particular episode will only attract budget travelers in California. If you're low on funds and stuck in Kentucky, you're not gonna drive to Big Sur for the weekend. We'll hopefully inspire plenty of people to put Big Sur on their bucket list—and don't get me wrong. There needs to be more than one reason to watch us. Travel programs draw crowds from all over, so it's not that. But if we're always based in LA, the episodes will only take us so far before our hundred bucks are gone."

Okay, I was with him. I was pretty sure.

"You wanna use different cities as home base," I stated.

"Exactly. So in the beginning, when we show that flyover footage and introduce the concept, we can be like, and this week, we're in Los Angeles, and we wanted to get out of the city for a weekend—blah, blah, blah. And then in the second episode, we could mix things up, maybe use Seattle as the starting point, and then we'll do a weekend in the Olympic Peninsula. Or we start off in Denver, and we go camping in the mountains."

Fuck, I wouldn't mind that last one. Camping in Colorado sounded fantastic to me.

He made a valid point too. We should have a new origin city with each episode.

"The problem is money," he finished.

I nodded again. It always fucking was.

I had an uncomfortable solution I'd been considering for a few weeks already, and I might have to drag Roe along with me. "When I first came out here, I met a guy whose brother runs a nightclub in West Hollywood. I was offered a job as a bartender —with the promise of insane tips—and if you want, if you really wanna go all in on this project, I can talk to him about getting you a job there too. By the sound of things, it won't be a problem."

Supposedly, we could make over five hundred bucks a night in just tips.

Roe tilted his head, a curious smile playing on his lips. "That sounds too good to be true—and you look like you're about to be sick."

No. Fuck that. It was just...

I cleared my throat and shifted in my seat. "It's a gay club."

"And?"

And? That was his reaction? Christ. *Now* I was uncomfortable. "And I'm not into dudes, fucking obviously. Are *you?*"

His eyebrows went up. "No, but—what the fuck does that have to do with anything? We're not gonna bend over, are we? It's just bartending?"

"Well, yeah..." But that didn't faze him one bit? I'd been as prepared as I could be, coming out here. I knew people were more...alternative...in California. Not everyone was raised going to church every Sunday like I was. Gay communities existed all over. I was fine with that. I didn't care. People could love or fuck whomever they wanted—and unlike my parents, I didn't believe it was sinful or unnatural.

At the same time, I could not, for the fucking life of me, shake this crazy unease whenever I was near a gay person. They put me on edge, made me feel out of sorts, almost flustered— which pissed me off. Nikki had several gay friends, and a couple of them liked to flirt with me just because of how awkward I got.

Roe leaned forward a bit and leveled me with a look. "Soon as we get home, make the damn call, Jake. I've heard what those bartenders can make if they're hot enough. I have *no* problem flashing my abs and a grin or two if it means we can head off to Denver in a couple weeks and do a second episode."

Flashing his—

For chrissakes.

"All right." I furrowed my brow and used my soggy sandwich as a distraction. I unwrapped the damn thing and...just resigned myself to accept a job where I'd be surrounded by drunk dudes horny for other dudes.

I supposed I shouldn't be surprised Roe was at ease. He was from New York and had studied journalism at NYU. Who fucking knew what people he'd been exposed to there.

When I glanced up, I found him smirking at me.

"You told me you were from Norfolk, right?"

I nodded once.

"Military town," he noted. "Technically in the South. Conservative folks, or...?"

I wouldn't go that far. Traditional, sure. Religious, absolutely. "After Clinton, my ma banned political talk around the house, but I know my old man voted for Obama, so..." I shrugged and took a bite from my sandwich. "What about you?" It was easier to turn the spotlight back on him.

He chuckled and scratched his nose. "My whole family's Catholic—the cherry-picking kind. Good for guilting your kids into attending mass and not cursing at the dinner table, but they're hella open-minded. I have a cousin who's gay and a cousin's son who's bi."

Oh. Yeah, there was none of that in my family. I had a hazy memory of seeing something when I was like eight or nine—I couldn't remember what it was or where I'd been—but I did recall my mother's reaction. I could still hear the angry tremor in her voice when she... I frowned to myself. Had I been holding something? And she'd ripped it away from me? I didn't know. It didn't matter. Or what she'd said. She'd just been furious with me, and I'd been so shocked, frozen by fear, because my ma rarely raised her voice.

It'd had something to do with homosexuality, though. I knew that much. I'd gotten a lecture and a punishment. And after that, the topic hadn't existed in my family.

Four days later, I was rethinking everything that'd led up to this moment. What I wanted to do was head back to the studio lab on campus and continue editing our material from Big Sur. I'd gotten hooked on our premise, on the easy humor Roe had added, everything we'd seen, and just the feeling of putting it all together on a computer. I'd fucking found what I wanted to do for the rest of my life. And instead, I was here, in a gay nightclub in WeHo, about to mix drinks with lewd names.

The doors opened in fifteen minutes.

"This is fucking brilliant," Roe laughed.

I didn't know about brilliant...

Ten of the most common cocktails had been given dirty names, and each one was scribbled on a small whiteboard behind the bar, so we could see the recipes clearly but the patrons could not. Sure, it would make for easy mixing for the untrained bartender like myself—though, I had practiced at home relentlessly the past two days. But I would still spend the night hearing "Give me a Hard Cock!" and "I'll have a Double Penetration!"

Thank fuck we had two experienced bartenders with us. I listened to them prattle on about the register—the card reader was wonky sometimes—which alcohol brands were default unless a customer had a request, advice on how to handle pushy patrons—

"And whatever you do, don't let them dictate your pace, sweetie," Juan said. "Make no mistake—you gotta be on your feet and work fast. Three hundred men will fill this place within the hour, and we only have two bars, but you don't let them rush you. Keep your cool and don't hesitate to be their authority. They eat that shit right up. Tell them to heel or simmer the fuck down, and the twinks will eat out of your hand. Okay, sweetie?"

Sure, sweetie.

I had half a mind to call my mother and apologize. I didn't even know for what.

"I got it." I nodded firmly. While I was definitely over-whelmed and unsettled, authority wasn't a problem. I wasn't insecure by nature, and I had no issues putting my foot down.

Improvise, adapt, overcome.

Oorah.

Two minutes before the doors opened, the DJ took to the stage in the back of the club, and the whole place lit up. What'd once been black and nondescript, from floors to ceiling, became an electric light show in purple, green, and blue.

"Have a good hunt tonight!" One of the bartenders I hadn't been introduced to crossed the dance floor to get to the bar on the other side.

"Are you kidding me?" Juan laughed. "We have the straight guys over here. We're going home rich."

I flicked a glance at Roe, and he smirked. He'd shared a theory on the way here tonight—that straight men drew their own crowd in a gay club. Something about a fantasy chase. Was he right? Was that a thing? Was that why we'd been hired on the spot?

"Sixty seconds!" someone hollered.

Roe and I stayed in the background as instructed. The first hour, we'd take orders through Juan and Ricky.

I rolled my shoulders, mildly uncomfortable in my tee. It was a simple black T-shirt, but it was a size or two too small. I could guess the reason...

At least I felt right at home in my own jeans, and nobody had told me I couldn't wear my ball cap. I kept it on backward, as usual.

Roe was a jeans-and-tee kind of guy too.

"Opening the doors!"

Right as someone uttered those words, music began pouring out into the club, and Juan poured five shots of vodka. He handed Ricky one, downed one himself, extended one to Roe, and I got two.

Huh?

"You look like you need an extra." He winked.

Heh. Maybe he was right.

I threw back the first, then the second, and made a face as the taste burned its way down my throat. Vodka wasn't necessarily my poison, but I wasn't too picky. Not on a night like this anyway.

Let's make some money.

People swelled in like an expanding sponge, and the first drink orders came shortly after. It was eleven o'clock, so guests were arriving in various states of intoxication, whether they'd slammed drinks at home or come from a bar. I was put on two-ingredient patrol, presumably because Roe fit right in where I didn't. He'd bartended a little bit in college, and he was a social butterfly. He didn't stay in the background for long before Ricky brought him up to the front line.

It was comfortable in the back, where I mixed gin and tonics, vodka cranberries, Cuba Libres, Jack and Cokes, screwdrivers, and martinis. But that wasn't why I was here. If I kept my back to the club the whole night, I'd go home almost as poor as I'd been when I'd arrived.

Get it together.

I heard Roe laugh at something over the pumping music, and I looked over at him. He was talking—or yelling—with a patron at the same time as he was mixing what looked like a negroni.

For fuck's sake. Why was I so chickenshit? Clearly, I needed this crash-course edition of exposure therapy. It wasn't like the guests were gonna crawl over the bar and attack me. Hot guys were a dime a dozen; I wasn't some grand prize. If anything, I was ridiculous.

I blew out a breath and closed my eyes temporarily. *Come on.* I could fake it at the very least. I wasn't such a homebody that I couldn't enjoy a night out. I was even a decent dancer, and I didn't mind pop music—despite that I preferred rock, both the hard variety and the country variety.

A Katy Perry remix morphed into a Lady Gaga remix, one of Nikki's favorite songs. By the look of it, Roe was a fan too. But I already knew that. Having spent fifteen hours on the road with him, I didn't need him to tell me he liked pop stars and dance music.

After bringing Juan the last four gin and tonics and one Jack and Coke, I asked him to promote me to three-ingredient cocktails and a bit more customer interaction.

"On one condition!" he hollered. With a wicked grin, he poured me two more fucking shots. "You gotta loosen up, sweetie!"

"Buddy, how many shots did you do tonight?"

I didn't wanna think about it. I swallowed against the nausea crawling up my throat and rolled down the window. "They seemed like a good idea at the time."

Gay men had bought me drinks tonight. I hadn't declined as much as I should have.

I groaned and leaned closer to the window, and Roe drove like a fucking lunatic.

Fucking hell, I couldn't close my eyes for a second unless I wanted to throw up in his truck. My skin prickled uncomfortably, I was running hot and cold, and saliva pooled in my mouth like it did before I got sick.

"We're almost at your girl's place," he told me. "Think you can last five minutes?"

"We'll just have to see, won't we?" I muttered. "For the record, I'm nothin' like a condor. Condors don't get drunk and work for tips."

He chuckled. "Okay."

But I still liked the comparison. I'd been editing that footage today, with Roe's rambling about the condors, and it'd stuck. I'd even read up on the bird on Wikipedia.

"Did you know they mate for life?" Shit, I heard the slurring in my voice. I needed to sober the fuck up. The world was spinning too quickly, and all the traffic lights blurred into a hazy mush of green and red.

"I did."

I blinked, feeling dizzy, and glanced over at him. And I wanted to make something crystal clear here. Because this dude... He was a good guy. I liked him. He was passionate, and we should continue working together.

"We could go into business together," I said. "If this pilot thing doesn't work out, we could release it on our own. Everyone has their own YouTube show these days. I've seen it. I mean, some of them. Some shows. Not about condors but other shit."

He grinned but said nothing at first, focused on maneuvering us through the late-night traffic. Or early morning. I didn't fucking know. The club had closed at two, and we'd had work to do once the door was locked.

"We can certainly discuss it when you're sober," he answered. "But it's gonna work. We have a good idea. And YouTube won't get me off the streets anytime soon."

About that...

I squinted out the window, recognizing where we were. Nikki's place was just around the block. "Crash on our couch," I yawned. Oh fuck, that felt good. Yawning felt *amazing*. Did condors yawn? "I talked to Nikki about it earlier. She's okay with it."

Nikki was very understanding that way. She was a good egg. Generous and supportive. The fuck she was doing with me was unclear, but I'd pay her back. According to Roe, I was a condor, and I didn't get by without a little help from my friends.

That was a song, wasn't it? I was sure it was.

Either way, I'd never let Nikki forget how much she'd helped me.

Noticing that Roe hadn't answered me, I looked over at him again.

He hesitated. "Are you sure?"

I frowned. Of-fucking-course I was sure. "I wouldn't have offered if I wasn't."

He exhaled and smiled uncertainly. "I'm in no position to turn down a couch and the option to shower in the morning— and it wouldn't be for long. We're working every night this week, so I'm thinking by Monday, I'll be able to afford a motel."

I waved a hand, dismissive. If that's what he wanted to do, sure. He'd definitely made more money than me tonight, but I was still happy with my four hundred bucks. I was gonna give half of it to Nikki and save the other half for Colorado.

Did they have condors out there?

"Do they have condors in Colorado?" I wondered.

"Jesus Christ, man," he laughed. "Let's get you to bed." By sheer luck, he found parking fairly close to Nikki's building.

As soon as he'd killed the engine, I tumbled out and felt my stomach lurch and revolt. My God, I was never drinking again, for at least a week. I pressed a fist to my mouth and wondered if I should just throw up now or upstairs.

I might end up passed out on the bathroom floor.

Once Roe had grabbed some essentials, I aimed for the stairs to Nikki's apartment on the second floor. It took Herculean strength, but I fucking got there. Then I was digging out my keys and slumping against the door because balance was a tricky thing.

Somewhere out on the street, a dog barked. I didn't look

because I was concentrating on getting the key into the lock, and it worked on the fourth or eleventh try.

"Thank you for your patience," I said politely.

Roe found that funny.

I pushed the door open and steadied myself against it, and then I almost tripped over one of Nikki's shoes. Her deathtrap heels were littered across the floor like part of an obstacle course.

I made a sweeping motion with my foot to clear a path before I kicked off my own shoes and let Roe in. The whole place was dark, and I assumed Nikki was asleep down the hall.

It was just a one-bedroom, so there wasn't much to show Roe, and he had no issues finding the couch in the living room right in front of us.

He clapped me on my shoulder. "Get some rest, man. We'll talk in the morning."

I nodded. "Help yourself to anythin' in the fridge—but I'd stay away from the juice. Nikki puts spinach in that shit."

He chuckled quietly. "Duly noted. Thanks for letting me crash here."

"No problem." I yawned and wished him a good night, then made my way down the hall. I'd go to the bathroom soon, but I just needed to lie down for a minute first.

The bedroom was dark and quiet, with just enough moonlight revealing Nikki's sleeping form under the covers.

A wave of exhaustion washed over me as I slumped down on the edge of the bed.

I managed to haul my tee over my head, but that was as far as I got. I couldn't strip off my jeans. I was already sitting down. They would simply have to stay on.

I groaned under my breath and scrubbed my hands over my face.

Christ, what a night.

I heard faint rustling behind me, followed by Nikki's sleepy voice. "You're home."

"Mm." I reached behind me blindly and patted her hip. "Go back to sleep, hon."

You're home... Her short phrase replayed in my head, and I wondered if I had imagined the rasp in—but no. She sniffled, which jostled me a bit out of my drunken state. Was something wrong?

I turned around and squinted in the darkness. "You okay?"

She sniffled again. "I don't know," she whimpered. "I'm pregnant, Jake."

She was fucking what?

CHAPTER 2
2011

"Grandma, lemme help you." I hurried around the truck to help her out. The woman wasn't even five feet tall; she could break something just stepping off a curb.

"I am quite capable, you know." She sniffed indignantly but still grabbed on to my hand as she climbed out of my truck. "My, my, this is a busy neighborhood. Can Colin sleep with all this noise?"

I smiled. "He sleeps just fine."

After grabbing her luggage, I offered my arm, and she linked hers with mine. I was stupidly happy to have her here, and I hoped she liked my new place. Culver City was an upgrade, for sure. So was my choice of roommate. I just preferred to live with Roe. He was less prone to throwing shoes at me.

We'd been offered this apartment in the nick of time, about two weeks after Nikki had dumped my sorry ass. According to her, I was the most uninvolved, boring, and passive boyfriend ever to exist. But I was a good dad, so we still got along somewhat.

Nikki wasn't entirely wrong. Other than being there 100% for pregnancy-related things, I was the douchebag who'd prioritized work. She'd lasted until Colin was three months old before she'd told me to get the fuck out.

The walk to the apartment wasn't long, and soon, Grandma and I took the elevator up to the third floor. It was an old factory-like red-brick building, with vaulted windows and a courtyard with a pool—which was nice in the August heat. We had a balcony too. Not to mention the absolute smallest apartment in the building. But Roe and I didn't care. He didn't have to sleep in his truck, and I could at least say I was supporting myself financially. And my son, of course.

Upon entering the apartment, I did a quick scan and tried to see the place through Grandma's eyes. The big window in the living room—and the bedroom, for that matter—helped make our home look more furnished than it was. Roe and I had gone all out with a big pullout couch, flat-screen, coffee table, and bed, and...that was pretty much it. I'd bought a nightstand and a dresser right before Grandma's arrival, so that was waiting for her in the bedroom. I'd assembled them last night.

We only had a kitchenette, which didn't bother us. We didn't cook much, and now we didn't have to worry about furniture there either.

When my sister had come out for a week a couple months ago, she'd helped me hang curtains. She'd hung some pictures on the walls too. Pictures I'd taken over the years. But I appreciated the curtains more because it got incredibly bright around ten, when the sun shone right in.

"Remind me, darlin'—where's your friend going to sleep?"

"At his girlfriend's," I replied. "Let's take your luggage to the bedroom so you can get settled. I put clean sheets on the bed for you."

I knew she didn't quite understand our living arrangement. That was fine. We had to be creative in a tiny one-bedroom apartment. Then again, both Roe and I had arrived in LA empty-handed. There was nothing his or mine at our place. We'd bought everything together, and so we shared our space too. When I had my boy here every other week, the bedroom was mine. When it was Nikki's week, the bedroom was Roe's.

"It's a very nice place, dear. But quite small." She patted my arm.

"It's temporary." I opened the door to the bedroom and let her in first. "We hope to buy a house next year."

She peered up at me through her Ruth Bader Ginsburg glasses. "You could start with a crib for your son."

I chuckled. Helpful advice filed away and forgotten. My little bear didn't need a crib. He slept next to me.

After showing her how to work the curtains and where the bathroom was, across the hall, I gave her some privacy so she could take a nap. Flying all the way from Florida had tuckered her out, and that suited me fine.

Nikki would be here any minute to drop Colin off, and I'd rather not introduce her to my grandmother. For some reason, she'd never approved of my girlfriends, much less my exes.

While I waited, I put on coffee and hauled out Colin's stuff from the hallway closet. At ten months old, he was a fast little shit, crawling and scooting all over the place. He wasn't walking yet, but he could stand fine, and he liked to headbang to Uncle Roe's music.

I couldn't fucking lie. As overwhelming as it'd been to first come to grips with becoming a dad, and then experiencing the first few months with a newborn...I'd found a love that surpassed all others, that couldn't be expressed with words, and that filled me with life. Roe had noticed the changes first. How I'd almost become someone else, and I guessed I saw it now too.

I may have been an unengaging boyfriend, but I fucking loved being my kid's dad.

To be honest, it was a little bit Roe too. No matter how small our apartment was, I was in a good place in life. I'd come out to LA with nervous hopes, and now I had a son and a best friend. Not too shabby. Work was picking up too. Our hopes had morphed into realistic goals.

I tossed some of Colin's toys on the couch, a couple on the floor, and placed his second favorite blanket on the coffee table. He loved to reach for stuff, and the coffee table was essentially his place to shine. He used it to steady himself when he bounced and eyed the next destination to explore.

When the coffee was ready, I poured myself a mug and double-checked the fridge. Weaning the boy off formula and breast milk had forced me to learn some basic cooking, but he made it easy for me. Everything was overcooked, and then I just threw it all in a blender.

He had no complaints.

Maybe I wouldn't have to buy formula again. He was down to one bottle a day, and I'd picked up a big box at Costco last time.

The doorbell finally rang, and I stalked out of the kitchenette and toward the entryway around the corner. I smiled as I heard Colin babbling on the other side of the door.

And there he was.

"Bam-ba-ba-bam!"

I grinned and reached out when he did the same. "How's my bear? Huh? Good to see Daddy?"

He laughed and pushed my cheeks together.

"Is Daddy as adorable as you now?" I snarled playfully and smooched his chubby face.

Nikki smiled indulgently and handed over Colin's diaper bag. "Brace yourself for a clingy boy. I think he's entered the separation anxiety phase."

Oof. We'd read about that.

"Good to know." I positioned Colin on my hip, dropped the diaper bag on the floor, and accepted the stroller next. She'd folded it together already. "You want coffee?"

"I'm afraid I gotta run. I have work." She closed the distance between us and pressed kisses to Colin's cheeks. "You be good for Daddy now, sweetie. I love you so much."

I smiled as he smooched her back and gave her the cute growling sound that'd earned him my nickname for him.

Then she took a step back and righted her purse over her shoulder. "By the way, do you think we can get together soon and record more bedtime stories?"

"Yeah, of course." That was a good plan. I was running low too.

The new iPad had released the day after my birthday this year, so I'd splurged. It was our way to stay connected with Colin when it wasn't our week. We'd filmed each other reading bedtime stories, so Colin would get story time with Mama on the iPad this week.

"When did he eat?" I lifted him up and gave his butt a sniff. No need to change yet, at least.

"He's good till dinner," she answered.

"Wo-wa-bam!" Colin babbled.

"I'm in total agreement with you, buddy." I nodded firmly.

Nikki laughed softly and stepped out into the hall. "I'll go before my own separation anxiety kicks in." Yeah, that one was fucking real. I knew the feeling. "We'll talk, Jake. Bye, you two."

"Definitely. Have a good one, hon. Wave to Mama, Bear."

He did like to wave.

Before long, it was just the two of us, and we spent the next hour playing on the living room floor. I plugged the iPad into a charger, too, and read Nikki's notes for the week. No major developments, though we tended to call each other for those. He'd gotten fussy about mashed bananas, but that could be a fluke, according to Nikki. We'd just have to see.

"Wawr!"

I chuckled and folded an arm under my head as he climbed on top of me and growled.

It was possible I'd fallen asleep right here on the floor a couple times.

Every now and then, he'd tune in to the music playing on the stereo—kept fairly low so it wouldn't wake up my grandmother—and that was when he started bouncing and bobbing his head.

Sometimes, I still couldn't believe I'd helped create this little person. Christ—even when he drooled on my damn face. I groaned and laughed and wiped at my cheek. Which he found hilarious.

Since the day he was born, my mom had demanded weekly updates, and it'd led to another kind of story time. She'd started opening old photo albums and loved to tell me how Colin was just like me. She'd compared baby pictures too. Sure, the resemblance was there, but he took after Nikki as well. Colin's eyes were slowly taking her green shade, and the temper sure as fuck didn't come from me.

Since I didn't know Nikki's natural hair color, I had nothing to go on there. Colin's messy little mop was almost as dark as mine.

At the sound of keys turning in the lock, I tilted my head toward the door and spotted Roe coming through with his arms full of...I didn't even know. Five big boxes.

"Baaa-wow-bam! Uck!" Colin yelled.

"Yeah, it's Uncle Roe."

"Hey!" Roe smiled and kicked the door shut.

I sat up, and Colin tumbled down my front before he began his speedy crawl toward Roe.

"What the hell is all that?" I asked.

"A good fuckin' bargain is what this is," he said proudly. "A table and four chairs for the balcony—they were half off because it was some display item. Let's assemble them before dinner. Is your grandma here yet?"

I nodded and got to my feet. "She's restin'." I picked up the pace when Colin blocked Roe's path, and I threw my boy over my shoulder. A table and four chairs, huh? We'd talked about buying a grill for the balcony, but this made more sense as a first step. Roe would undoubtedly collect brownie points with my grandmother too, because my plan had been for us to either go out or sit on the couch.

In my defense, it was a big couch.

All right, it was a good purchase.

I could suddenly see myself spending many late nights out here on the balcony with Roe and Colin. The noise from the courtyard was nothing in comparison to the traffic and food trucks on the outside of the building; now we were just one of the handful of residents having dinner with friends and family. A couple kids were in the pool while their parents used the barbecue area down there, and someone's cat was wailing in an open window.

I grabbed another quesadilla from one of the food containers and leaned back again. Colin was asleep on my chest—a bit early, but it was fine. He usually slept through the night anyway.

I didn't say much, too content to watch Roe and Grandma across from me. Safe to say, Roe was a crowd-pleaser. Grandma had already insisted he call her Grandma Josephine.

I was just so fucking at ease, I couldn't find the right word for it.

"In that case, I've seen all the episodes," Grandma summarized. "My favorite was when y'all went to North Carolina, of course. I was born there, as you know. It's more than the Outer Banks."

I smiled. That'd been a fun episode. I'd obviously given her a shout-out, because it was her advice we'd taken on where to go. Which had sort of become the secondary concept of *The Hundred-Dollar Nomads*. We ventured off the beaten paths and showed hidden gems often missed by tourists. Big Sur had obviously been our exception.

"Way more," Roe agreed, reaching for the nachos. "That was a good trip. Even if Jake doesn't remember much."

I chuckled. "Can you blame me?"

"Unfortunately, not one bit." He winked. He turned to Grandma next. "Your grandson is a damn wizard behind the camera, but I need him in front of it too."

Heh. I was working on it. A lot had changed. Becoming some sort of actor would have to be dealt with in baby steps. At most, I was a decent sidekick and made frequent appearances with minimal interaction.

Last year had been too much of a whirlwind. Just a couple weeks after Nikki had told me she was pregnant, Roe's network connection had come through. Our pilot had been picked up, and we'd been contracted for six episodes. Between ultrasounds and holding Nikki's hair when she'd vomited, Roe and I'd had to fly across the country on a tiny budget to put together our show in a mad rush.

Getting that confirmation—hearing those words that someone had picked up our pilot—wasn't all sunshine and roses. That *deal* didn't automatically mean a network wanted to invest a lot of money in you. But we'd fucking shown them, and now we were in preproduction for season two. Twelve episodes. A slightly bigger budget. More support.

"I did notice you have wonderful chemistry on the show," Grandma said with a thoughtful nod. "Viewers like that, darlin'. That's entertainment."

"*Exactly*. She gets it." Roe was a fan of Grandma. "We get our highest ratings when Jake and I joke around."

I smirked around a mouthful of food and shook my head. I was fucking working on loosening up! I'd told him plenty. Hell, I'd promised the new producer I would appear more. It was in my contract.

Grandma eyed me in her pensive way, which could unsettle me if I wasn't so relaxed. She'd always been able to read me better than my own parents.

"The thing about Jake," she said, facing Roe again, "is to lure him out using his own passions. That's how you get him excited and eager to talk."

I was fairly certain that applied to everyone on this planet.

"So what are his passions?" Roe got curious. "In the year and a half I've known him, he's dedicated himself one hundred percent to filming, editing, being a daddy, taking *countless* photos of Colin, paying the bills as soon as we receive them, and studying technology."

Hey, I was a good bartender now too.

"Well, they change, you see," Grandma answered. "When he was little, he would help me in the garden every summer. He loved roses. Then his grandfather gave him a camera, and he started taking pictures of the roses. Which then became photos of trees, animals, and..." She lifted a brow at me. "Do you remember what came next?"

I nodded with a dip of my chin. "Aircraft and ships." Since I was from Norfolk, the military had always been close by.

"Then he became a Marine," Roe murmured.

Grandma nodded. "Now I think he's reverted a fair bit. He loves nature, doesn't he? You can tell by the way he films."

They didn't *have* to talk as if I weren't here.

"He hasn't made a single friend out here," Roe continued. "But he'll greet every dog that runs up to him."

I dipped down and brushed my lips to the top of Colin's head. "Damn. I thought you were my buddy."

Roe grinned. "Aside from me."

Well, I didn't want a lot of people in my life. I was happy with what I had.

"Jake can be a tough nut to crack," Grandma noted. "You just have to look for different topics. Eventually, you'll find somethin' that'll break the levees."

Typical of Roe to see that as a challenge.

All my life, I'd heard that I didn't talk enough. I was too introspective. Kept to myself a lot. Wasn't passionate about others. Rarely got excited. Didn't take much initiative. And I didn't know. Maybe there was something wrong with me.

Sometimes it actually felt like that, especially when I dated. I'd never once pursued a woman. They'd pursued me, and I'd been content to go along for the ride for however long it lasted. I'd read about love; I'd seen fellow Marines talk about their wives and family members with longing in their eyes, but I hadn't been able to relate until the day Colin was born.

My absolute favorite moment with him was every morning we woke up together. He'd stretch out and make that adorable growling sound, then blink sleepily and see me lying next to him, and he'd cuddle close to me.

What the fuck else did I need?

Grandma and Roe changed the topic shortly after. Grandma was curious about our next adventures, and Roe was happy to divulge. He told her about our upcoming travels and about his hope that he and I would start a podcast together. Business-wise, I knew that would be a fantastic move, but who in their right mind would wanna listen to me talk about...what?

Roe and Grandma had topics lined up, it seemed like. They moved on to discuss her stay here, and she was very much looking forward to visiting the Santa Monica Pier, the tar pits, and the Hollywood Walk of Fame. She invited Roe to join us, but he regretfully declined. We'd been working so much, and he'd promised his girlfriend he'd spend some time with her.

"I'm actually supposed to be at her place now," he chuckled.

"How long have you been together?" Grandma wondered.

"About two months," Roe replied. "We'll see how long it lasts. She thinks I work too much. She complains that I spend more time with Jake than with her."

I grinned against Colin's soft hair and kept brushing kisses on his head.

"Back in my day, I would never say this, but you're both young," Grandma told us. "You have an exciting future ahead of you if you keep working on your show—and other ventures." That one earned me another cocked brow. "I would like to sell your autographs on eBay before I develop dementia."

I choked on a chuckle. *Jesus Christ, Grandma.*

"I love this lady," Roe laughed. "Did Jake tell you our show has its own Wikipedia page now?"

"He told me the other day." Grandma patted Roe's arm. "You best believe I brag about you at the club. That's my grandson and his friend, I say. Maggie's always going on and on about her Wall Street grandson—but I sure shut her up."

And who was there to shut Grandma up? Absolutely nobody. An unstoppable force, that one.

One of the first things that'd developed naturally when I'd become a father was the infamous dad radar. I slept *well*, really well, and still, the moment Colin stirred in his sleep, I woke up momentarily just to make sure everything was all right. So when I roused one night at the sound of something rustling, I automatically expected to find my boy rolling over. Except, the sound came from the hallway.

I squinted in the dark.

Colin was fast asleep between two pillows, his pajama shirt riding up to reveal his belly, one hand clutching his blanket, the light covers twisted between his legs.

I righted the covers and tucked him in on instinct, and then I heard something again.

The front door opened just as I flicked on the flashlight on my phone, and it was Roe. Not that I'd expected anyone else. He'd come home in the middle of the night before.

Trouble in paradise again?

"Ignore me," he whispered. He kicked off his shoes, then ducked into the kitchen and opened the fridge.

Kinda hard to ignore him, though. Where did he think he was gonna sleep? I wasn't taking Grandma back to the airport till tomorrow, and he knew that.

Roe reemerged with a bottle of Coke and walked past the couch. "Go back to sleep." He opened the balcony door and stepped outside.

I scrubbed a hand over my face and dragged myself up. Go

back to sleep—yeah, right. I pulled on a pair of sweats, cast a glance at Colin, and then headed out to see what was up.

The air was fucking nice at this hour. I couldn't blast the AC a whole lot with Colin next to me, so the breeze that met me in the dark of the balcony felt good.

Roe lit up a smoke and sat down at the table.

Something had to be wrong. He only smoked when he was drunk, and he didn't appear lit.

"You okay?" I asked quietly.

He leaned back and exhaled some smoke skyward. "That's the problem, innit? I don't even care she broke up with me."

There we had it.

Maybe Grandma was right. Maybe we should just focus on work. We had so much going on, and our schedules were difficult to sync as it was. I had Colin every other week, we had our show, and we had our bartending gig. All the money we'd made from the network had been invested, so we still needed to pay rent somehow. And childcare and insurance and...fuck, the list went on.

Thankfully, we didn't need to rent studio time anymore. That'd been an expensive journey. Now we had a production company covered by the network, and that was another thing. Roe and I had discussed starting our own production company, something that would require even more time.

"Dating will have to wait," Roe sighed.

"Maybe it's for the best."

He nodded slowly, then cracked a little grin. "I kinda want a kid of my own. I think that's why I rushed into things with Vanessa."

Oh.

Yeah, I guessed that made sense, in retrospect. He came from a big family, and he'd mentioned wanting kids one day. I just hadn't thought it would be anytime soon.

I cleared my throat. "You know I wouldn't change anythin' in how I ended up with Colin, but last year was rough. You were right there next to me. Waiting a couple years till we're more settled probably won't hurt you."

He chuckled silently. "You sound like my cousin."

"Which one?" When we'd recorded an episode outside New York last winter, Roe had introduced me to two of them. Angus and Cullen. There were a few others, all significantly older.

"Greer—I talked to him earlier." Roe yawned. "He's back stateside and called me. I'd had a few, so I told him how things were going and that I wanted a family. Like, I wanna have roots. I wanna feel that..." He struggled to find the words. "That true *coming home* feeling."

I knew exactly what he was talking about. A feeling that'd eluded me before Colin.

"He told me to build a home first." Roe smirked faintly. "Focus on work, get our business off the ground, and then I can fill a house with ankle biters and afford to feed them too."

I smiled. Spoken like a true jarhead. Prepare, prepare, prepare.

Taking another puff from his cigarette, Roe leaned forward and got serious. "Here's the thing, Jake. I believe we can go really fuckin' far—but you have to want it too."

The gravity of what he said hit me, and rather than confirming I did want this, I kept my mouth shut.

Because he wasn't done. "Now's the time for us to push. Our first season did well enough for the network to want a longer second season, and we can help get the ratings up even more. You read the comments yourself—people think we're funny together. Those who had less interest in the destination kept watching because we were entertaining."

Fuck, this was sobering. A heart-to-heart at, what, four in

the morning? Business-related or not, this was Roe reaching out to me.

"What do you suggest?" I asked. "You wanna do the podcast?"

"Yeah," he replied bluntly. "We have a modest audience to build on. We need to be on social media. We need to promote ourselves—and our show—and reveal who we are. So we'll be visible to more people, more potential viewers and listeners."

I'd already acknowledged to myself that he was right. I knew he was. He made perfect sense. It was just—I didn't fucking know what to talk about.

"You know what John and Ortiz said about the third season," he said.

I nodded once and started tapping my foot restlessly.

Of course I remembered. If we got green-lit for a third season, we'd discuss more than a new raise. That's when sponsors entered the picture. Sponsors were the big money.

Michael Ortiz had turned out to be a great producer, and he was less of a network suit than John. I appreciated that in a guy.

"I'm not a content creator," I said. "If I don't know what to talk about, I'm just not gonna do it. I ain't sayin' you need to feed me lines, but I'm not a natural in front of the camera. You know that."

"I actually think you're wrong, but we can discuss that later," he responded. "I will give you topics and talking points, Jake. Trust me. Let me work out a concept for us, some sort of theme, and then you can see for yourself."

Since I had no argument for why this wasn't a good idea, not even my own reluctance to be the center of attention, I agreed. And whatever he thought I was wrong about, he could keep to himself.

"We good?"

"Yup." I pressed record and joined Roe at our lunch spot for the day. The tailgate of our rental truck had been dropped, and he'd rolled out his sleeping mat across it for a comfy seat.

I was a pig in shit, to be honest. Surrounded by mountain ranges, prairies, and an open road. We were just off the side of it, and we hadn't seen anyone drive by in over an hour.

The trees were changing colors. The air was crisp. The sky was blue.

I bit into my sub, having looked forward to it all fucking morning. We'd bought them on the way, and mine was filled with turkey, cheese, lettuce, tomatoes, and some sauce that was un-fucking-believable. And the bread, fluffy and baked this morning. Heaven.

"So we're in Back Country, Wyoming, this weekend," Roe said. "No, wait. I didn't like that. Roll again."

When was he gonna learn? We didn't *roll*. We kept shooting, and I edited it all together later.

"We're in Back Country, Wyoming. Is that a good tone?"

I chewed and made a rolling motion. We needed alternates anyway. They were good for trailers and teasers we released online.

"Wait, I think I got it," he said. "Say you don't know where we are when I ask. We'll do it a few times, so mix up your replies."

I snorted and took another bite. All right. We'd used a similar angle before, and it'd been a crowd-pleaser, according to focus groups.

"Jake?"

"Yeah," I answered with my mouth full.

"Where are we?"

I straightened a bit and glanced out over the prairie. "I have no idea."

He scratched the side of his head, then brushed crumbs off his hoodie. New take. "Greetings from... I don't even know! When did we pass the last town?"

I checked my watch. "About three hours ago...?"

He nodded and looked into the camera. "That's as accurate as it's gonna get. We're in Back Country, Wyoming, this weekend."

I liked that one. The details would be added in editing later, our exact location and so on. As well as a list of cities we'd recommend originating from for this trip. So, if you had a hundred bucks to spend on a weekend, and you were from places like Salt Lake City, Billings, Denver, and a few others, this was a good budget journey.

"Do the listing thing now," he said. "Conversation-style?"

Yeah, that one was best. Less scripted and forced.

I chewed what was in my mouth and started ticking off Wyoming attractions. "Yellowstone."

"Of course. Grand Teton and Hot Springs."

I added two fingers. "Flaming Gorge, Buffalo Bill, and..." I trailed off and stopped counting.

"All fantastic sights—and obviously we're not doing any of them," Roe chuckled, facing the camera once more. "In this episode, Jake and I are hiking down a lesser-known canyon to spend the night in an actual ghost town."

"The way you say actual makes me worried you think there will be actual ghosts," I told him.

"No!" he laughed and shoved at me. I smirked. "But we have so many ghost towns in this country that've turned into tourist attractions—and this is one of those that hasn't. It's *actually* a ghost town. Completely abandoned."

His excitement was slightly foreboding, because I had hiked with Roe so many times now, and he wasn't the most careful fella. He'd fallen into a stream in Colorado, a creek in Texas, he'd twisted his ankle in Washington, and he'd almost torn down a hornet's nest in Oregon.

"You up-to-date on your tetanus shot?" I asked. "Because I see you falling through a roof or cutting up your leg on a rusty car."

He shook his head and addressed the camera. "He has so much faith in me."

The end of October and beginning of November was a stressful period that resulted in way too little sleep. We wrapped up our production and edited our entire second season in two weeks, Colin turned one, Roe and I started Two Condor Chicks Production, he launched us on social media—with a helpful promo push from the network—we were guests on a morning radio talk show to promote our show, and every available night was spent bartending in West Hollywood.

To say I was dead on my feet was the understatement of the year.

"I want you to memorize these numbers, Jake," Roe told me as we entered the nightclub. "Two thousand followers on Instagram, three thousand followers on Twitter, twelve thousand likes on our Facebook page—and tomorrow, we start our podcast. This is *it*, man. Shit's gonna explode from here on out."

Shit had exploded this morning when I'd changed Colin's diaper too.

Maybe *Variety* could write about *that*.

Or that, from now on, we had no bedroom. Because Roe had turned it into a podcast studio. The living room looked like a squatter's nest. We'd stopped turning the pullout back to a couch in the morning; we didn't fucking have time. And now the bed stood there too. It was a good thing Colin loved to bounce around on the mattress since we'd lost most of our floor space.

"You sure you want me to handle the Instagram account?" I asked. It looked like that social media platform was gonna explode, again, much like Colin's diaper. They'd gained five million users just in the last few months.

"You're the photographer. One post every day." He clapped me on the shoulder and ducked into the changing room. "When Haley gets here, we'll talk strategy. She sounds like a super genius on the phone. Unlike her big brother."

"Don't worry, she'll learn to dumb herself down for your sake one day, too, just like I did." I grinned to myself and opened my locker, where another too-small black T-shirt was waiting for me.

"Hilarious," Roe drawled.

I thought so.

It was gonna be nice to see my baby sister again. She'd almost burned herself out in college, pulling off one major, one minor, and two part-time jobs. We didn't quite know how we'd all fit in our apartment, but she was coming to stay for a few months, and she'd promised to help us with our social media presence. She'd studied marketing, so she should be good at it.

I removed my ball cap and hauled my Henley over my head.

Roe sucked his teeth and eyed me. "Remind me to start lifting weights. And cover the fuck up."

I laughed.

Juan entered a moment later, and someone had apparently pissed in his cereal.

"What's up, sunshine?" I asked.

"Ricky quit," he snapped. "Fucker met some rich guy and moved to New York."

Oh…kay, then. Good to know.

"I can tell you're very happy for him," Roe offered.

I killed my laughter and squirmed into my work tee.

An hour later, the DJ gave a shout-out to Roe and played a heavy-beat remix of Lady Gaga's "Bad Romance," much to my buddy's excitement. His grins were hella infectious, and it was impossible not to get caught up in his energy bubble. We worked like a well-oiled machine, manning our own bar these days, while Juan and Oliver were on the other side of the club.

I bobbed my head to the music and took a quick swig of water in between drink orders, then got cracking on mixing two whiskey sours. A regular signaled that he wanted another gin and tonic, and I nodded to him. The bar was crowded as fuck, and each shift was a workout. But that kinda worked in our favor. Roe and I had picked up on the behaviors that gave us more tips.

For instance, lifting my tee to wipe sweat off my forehead?

Killer.

Just removing my cap to run a hand through my hair did the trick sometimes.

Roe came over to me and held a shot of something to my lips, and I opened my mouth as he threw back his own shot too. Fuck, that was Jägermeister. Not my favorite. I chased it down with beer, then handed over the two whiskey sours to the guy with blue hair.

He was a flirt.

When he leaned across the bar, I did the same and tilted my head to hear what he wanted to say.

"You still straight, handsome?"

I grinned and shook my head at him. "*Incredibly*. Sorry."

"Me too." He smirked ruefully and handed me a fifty. "There's a drink for you too in there."

I winked and moved on to my next customer.

At one AM, everyone was hammered, and some were getting hammered in the bathrooms. Roe and I were pretty lit too, which tended to happen the first work shift after I'd had Colin for a week. We took an cab to work on Fridays for a reason.

The DJ blasted a new song that Roe also loved, "Hangover," with Flo Rida and some British star whose name I could never remember. But it was a good tune, one that made the whole club jump up and down in the electric light show.

The money rolled in, and the card reader ran hot.

I blew out a breath and threw off my ball cap. It was way too hot for that. The music pumped through me, and I was fucking relieved the people were too drunk to order complicated cocktails at this hour. We were slinging mostly shots, beer, and vodka with various sodas. Rum too. These men loved their rum.

"Jake!"

"In a minute!" I set the card reader in front of a customer, then poured two beers for another.

Roe came over to me with a drunk smirk and showed a blackboard we used for writing specials. I squinted and tried to focus on what he'd scribbled. Wait, what? Buy the bartenders a Tequila Licking?

Were they ever gonna fucking stop using lewd names for— hold on. Buy the bartenders a what?

"You game?" Roe yelled over the music. "Juan gave me the green light! Twenty bucks to the register, we keep the rest!"

I, uh... Lemme get this straight. Customers could pay a hundred bucks for Roe and me to take a tequila shot off each other? We'd lick salt off each other's necks, do the shot, then grab a lime wedge from between the other's lips.

Amusement trickled in, and I just couldn't believe him. I cracked up and leaned closer to him. "We're bartenders—not turnin' tricks!"

"What's the difference?!" he retorted.

Oh, for fuck's sake. I groaned a laugh, then just shrugged and sort of agreed. My brain was in that magical place where life was a party and I was happy to work with my best friend. We had so much fun together.

Roe got swept away by the music and held up the blackboard for everyone to see on his way to the spot where we hung the weekly specials. Then he removed the Hard Cock(tail) Special and hung the very new Tequila Licking, a "Roe & Jake Exclusive."

My buddy was fucked in the head.

Thank *God* he'd limited this thing to three shots per night.

Before we knew it, Juan squeezed himself to the front and slapped a hundred-dollar bill to the sticky bartop. "You know what I want, boys!"

In the flashing lights, Roe laughed so hard he could barely breathe, and I couldn't hold my glare for shit. Of-fucking-course Juan would get this started. The mayhem was deafening. Juan began chanting, "Lick, lick, lick!" to the beat of the song, and others were quick to chime in.

Fuck it. If this was gonna be a new thing during our shifts— and talk about easy money—we better sell it. I grabbed two shot glasses and a bottle of tequila, and I let out a sharp whistle for Roe to get into gear.

"Grab the limes and salt over there!" I hollered.

Was he fucking shy? No. But he wasn't as cocky as he usually was. His shit-eating grin held traces of something else. Almost as if he had the decency to be at least a little bashful about the whole ordeal.

It was kinda sweet, actually.

For the first time in our friendship, I felt the need to raise the bar and take charge, so as soon as he joined me with salt and limes, I was in control. I closed the distance between us and placed a lime wedge between his teeth. Then I slid my fingers into his damp hair at the back of his head and exposed his neck for me. I poured salt across his skin before I lifted one of the shots in a silent *cheers* at the crowd staring hungrily.

"We're gonna regret this." I spoke for only him to hear. Then I ducked down and licked his neck. From his neckline up to his ear. The shot followed; I tossed it back and swallowed, and a rush of liquid heat slithered through me. A new level of intoxication hit me. I felt Roe shudder against me, and I thought I heard him mutter *fuck*. But I wasn't sure. The music, the roar of the customers, faded into the background, and I leaned in and bit into the lime, sending trickles of juice down our chins. The strong flavors mixed, with the lime winning in the end, and then all I saw were the lime-juice-stained lips that belonged to Roe.

Okay, shit, we were standing a bit too close. I saw too much for my drunken state—as in, my vision was surprisingly sharp— and I didn't care enough to examine my behavior. But we'd just made eighty bucks, so that was something, eh?

Roe exhaled a sultry laugh and sent the patrons a flirty smirk. It was his turn, and he wasn't hesitating anymore. He gave me a lime wedge that I kept between my teeth, and I tilted my head so he could pour salt on my neck.

Why was he—fucking hell, he was slowing things down. He put his hands on my sides and licked my neck slowly, and I looked up at the ceiling and released a breath. I wasn't gonna analyze that feeling. I fucking wasn't. It'd been a year since I'd gotten laid, and that was the only reason I reacted to his soft, wet tongue tracing my neck.

When he eased off and took the shot, I lowered my gaze again and found him watching me. He leaned in and up a bit, and I met him halfway so he could bite the lime. He took it from me, causing me to chuckle. The amusement in his eyes helped me come back down to earth again.

So that was the night we added Tequila Licking to the repertoire.

Jesus fuck.

"Jesus fuck." I groaned and let my forehead meet the table.

I wanted *nothing* more than to go back to sleep. Nothing. Not a damn thing.

Instead, I was sitting in our new podcast studio after four hours of sleep. The chairs were comfortable, the table less so. It wasn't meant to be a pillow. I might leave it a bad review.

I might also still be drunk.

Tequila Licking, my fucking ass.

I'd like to say it would never happen again, but the money was so damn easy.

Three shots, two hundred and forty bucks.

If my math was correct, Roe and I had made over nine hundred bucks each last night.

"Look alive, bro!"

I winced as Roe entered the room and dumped something on the table.

I managed to lift my head, and I scrubbed my hands over my face. How the fuck was he so chipper? Was he on drugs? My ma had warned me. LA people did a lot of drugs.

I'd just barely had the energy to take a shower, dig out a pair of sweats, and then come in here and collapse into one of the chairs. Meanwhile, Roe had gone out and bought us breakfast. He flipped open a bakery box to reveal donuts, and that wasn't all. He'd bought coffee, juice, strawberries, and Gatorade too.

"I'll be right back," he said.

I grunted noncommittally and reached for the coffee with my name on it.

Oh God, that was so good. I closed my eyes and took another sip.

I hoped he didn't need better lighting. I'd drawn the curtains shut, so the only source of light came from the lamp on the lonely nightstand in the corner.

I heard him working the ice machine in the kitchen, so I asked him to bring me a glass of water.

"Already on it!"

I exhaled.

Maybe I would survive.

My chances were increasing, even more so when he returned with a bottle of painkillers too. I'd completely forgotten.

"Okay, I love you," I muttered.

"Score," he chuckled. "You just focus on resuscitating yourself while I go through my list."

Solid plan. It felt a bit weird to be on this side of the tech responsibility. I was usually the one who handled all that, but he'd insisted for the podcast. He wanted to learn more—and I could tell he'd researched a lot. He'd hooked us up with great microphones, he'd bought a new laptop, headphones, and software, and I'd caught him a few times trying things out.

As always, he brought good content to the table. I liked his ideas.

After downing a couple painkillers, I reached for a donut and prayed some sugar would help the headache fuck off. Grandma said the only cure for a hangover was time, but while we waited, it was okay to fool ourselves with whatever poison we preferred.

I put on a pair of headphones while Roe practiced his intro and messed around on the laptop.

I was glad we'd agreed to release five prerecorded episodes before we sat down again to decide when to do these live. I liked the option of editing. Even though it required more work, the production would be cleaner and better quality. Those were my two cents.

"Good morning, you're Off Topic with Roe Finlay and Jake Denver. I'm Roe, and Jake is hungover as hell. Can you give us a sound, buddy?"

I snorted softly and took a bite of the donut. "Insert retching noises," I joked lamely.

Roe grinned and leaned back in his seat. "Speaking of you devouring that donut, we were gonna discuss the latest focus-group results we got from the network."

Right. That was on today's agenda. He wanted to do that now? Before we did the podcast thing?

"How's that on the topic of donuts?" I asked. Then I thought of the title of the show and raised my brows. "If that's a joke on our podcast's name, it's terrible."

He chuckled and leaned forward again, and he pulled out a couple documents from between the pages of a magazine. "It's actually very on topic. I have it in writing right here—viewers like seeing Jake eat."

Get the fuck out.

It really said that? How was that a thing? Weren't they supposed to ask what people thought about the destinations we picked?

"What else does it say?" I asked. "That's insane."

He grinned and scanned the document. "It's definitely the most extensive research they've done so far." We hoped it was for a good reason. Ortiz had mentioned they spent time on the shows and hosts they wanted to invest in. "Apparently, you're endearing and hot in some scruff, but I should be clean-shaven. Viewers respond favorably to your digs about my lack of finesse, at the same time as they like that I come off as a beginner. There's a slight bump in ratings that might correlate to when we started listing our professions under our names during the intro."

That was interesting. It'd been Ortiz's idea to showcase that Roe was an investigative journalist and I was a combat photographer and filmmaker. Two titles that, for some reason, felt unearned. Perhaps not the former, but it wasn't as if I had a degree in filmmaking.

"But it was around the time you joined me in front of the camera more too," he added. "I think that plays a bigger role. They really like our dynamic. You're the calm, steady big brother with experience in the wild—verbatim, for the record—and I'm the energetic teacher who engages with viewers of all ages. There's actually a private note from Ortiz about a possibility to look into a future production geared toward children. That could be fun."

Yeah, maybe.

I wasn't ruling anything out. I'd come to grips with the fact that Roe and I would get more control once we were more established. In the meantime, we agreed to most suggestions from the network.

Ortiz believed we'd be green-lit for a third season too, at which point we'd get a film crew. He was already looking to fill two positions.

"Wouldn't it be fun to add a food segment to the show?" Roe mused. "It's sort of become a tradition that we eat lunch during the intro, but it's always the same sandwiches we either buy on the way or make ourselves. Instead, it could be a local culture thing. Like, we prepare a meal over open fire or wherever we are, and we interview a local about the recipe or something."

That didn't sound bad at all.

"Aside from the fact that we're worthless in the kitchen, I like it."

He laughed. "We can learn. We learned to process baby food for Bear—that's Jake's little boy. He recently turned one, and yeah, he absolutely loved my gift for him. More so than the gifts his parents gave him."

I narrowed my eyes at him. Was he fucking recording? Was this the podcast episode?

He just smiled at me.

"You fucker," I said.

He found that funny. "I'll just edit that out."

Jesus Christ, thanks for the heads-up.

"Don't give me that look," he chuckled. "I picked the best possible moment to do this. You're too hungover to get uncomfortable, and you eased into conversation naturally because you had no idea I was recording."

No, no, he was still a fucker.

I wasn't ready to admit he had a point.

"*Anyway.*" Roe smirked at me. "You're Off Topic with Roe Finlay and Jake Denver. I'm Roe, and Jake recently started a fun family tradition for us. As mentioned, we're absolute shit in the kitchen, so we tend to eat out a lot. And when we have Jake's son with us every other week, we wait with bated breath for Tuesdays and Thursdays, when the street we live on fills up with food trucks."

It was actually Friday too...

"Jake and I *love* to eat," Roe went on. "But you try going out with a buddy who's married to his camera—without me, we'd never actually eat anything. He's too busy taking photos of the food joints, and he's become somewhat of a star—"

"Oh, for chrissakes," I laughed. "That's a stretch."

"The hell it is! You're documenting LA culture—and the million tiny cultures within it—and they love seeing you. These are proud mamas and papas—and now, of course, trendsetters—who wanna show off their food traditions for Jake's camera. There's actually a running joke. They keep asking when Jake's coffee table book is coming out."

I grinned and shook my head.

"But it's a nice tradition, innit?" Roe smiled, genuine. "I got my little pseudo nephew climbing on me while his daddy takes photos, and then I find what we wanna eat that night, and we stuff our faces on a nearby park bench. It's the ultimate found-family moment for me. Makes it a lot easier when I miss my mad bunch on the East Coast."

Shit. When he said it like that, I felt it too. Found family was the correct term.

"Found family. I like that." I nodded. "I reckon that's what LA is about—in the background. When you're not chasing your next career goal, you gotta find the people you wanna spend the holidays with if you can't go home. Or if you don't want to." It was my turn to smirk. "No offense to my folks back home in Virginia."

Roe chuckled, probably thinking about the conversation we'd had the other week about Thanksgiving and Christmas. I was staying in LA by choice since my sister was coming out. Roe was flying home for Thanksgiving but would spend Christmas with us and Nikki.

"On that note, I've received a bunch of newsletters from our favorite food trucks, and some are doing holiday menus," Roe mentioned. "Do you have a recommendation for this episode?"

Right. That was gonna be one of my tasks.

"I do." I cleared my throat and reached for my coffee. "Since Roe bought me hangover breakfast this morning, it's only right I buy him dinner tonight, so I propose The Copper Pot. I think they're in Santa Monica tonight. They sling some of the best carnitas this town has to offer, and if you ask for a Roe Special— yeah, that's a thing—they'll give you extra lime and pickled jalapeños on their carnitas soft tacos. *Unbelievably* good."

"My mouth is watering, I fucking swear," Roe said.

"You gonna edit that out too?" I smirked.

"No, maybe we should just fucking curse like we always do." He huffed. "I don't know what I was thinking with the appropriate language. We ain't appropriate."

I laughed.

"Dada, bow! Bow!"

"I don't know what bow means, baby," I groaned through a chuckle. The boy had been at it all day—bow, bow, bow. But we had no clue what he meant. It couldn't be Roe, it wasn't his blanket or any of his stuffies, it wasn't his sippy cup, and it wasn't food.

"Is this bow, Colin?" Roe held up Colin's stuffed giraffe, and I watched the interaction in the rearview. Traffic was a mess, so it'd be a minute before we got to the airport.

"No!" Colin batted away the plush toy. He got huffy and stubbornly looked out the window instead.

I stifled a grin and exchanged a look with Roe in the rearview. Colin learning how to speak was *fun*. It'd taken Nikki and me a week to figure out that Woe—or whoa, as we'd initially interpreted the sound as—was Roe and up-up was a toy at his day care.

To be fair, we would've connected the dots between Woe and Roe a lot faster if he'd been around when Nikki and I had started pointing at things. But he'd been in New York for

Thanksgiving, so realization hadn't dawned until Colin and I had picked up Roe at the airport.

Now we were on our way to pick up my sister. She couldn't possibly be bow. We hoped. There was zero resemblance.

Not that many words stuck at this point. He'd be babbling incoherently for a while to come, with his favorite addition of "No." Mama, no. Dada, no. Nooooo.

"You wanna get In-N-Out on the way back?" Roe asked. "I'm hungry."

Yeah, so was I. "Sounds good." Haley liked that too.

Roe and I had spent the morning cleaning our place. We just couldn't have the whole bedroom go to waste as a podcast studio slash office, even though we used it in some capacity every day, so we'd bought a guest bed for one of the corners. Haley would sleep there, and we could use it for Colin's nap time too. The living room was still a squatter's haven, though we'd turned the pullout back into a couch.

It was a drag to fold and unfold every day because we'd bought the damn thing knowing full well we'd sleep in it often, so it had to be real comfortable. But we needed the space too. Leaving the mattress extended when Colin was around made him cranky as soon as he'd tired of jumping on the bed. He had to be able to run around a bit too.

We couldn't fucking wait to move, to be honest. We'd loved the place when we'd moved in, but now it was a tight fit. Roe and I kept investing in equipment for future productions, Colin was growing so quickly, and now with Haley moving in with us... Yeah, the next paycheck couldn't come soon enough.

"By the way, since you're dating again, I just wanna say hands off my sister," I told Roe. It wasn't me being a chauvinistic asshole; I just didn't want drama in my own home. In my own, very tiny home. "Haley's already expressed you're hot as fuck, so not only does she have poor taste in men, but you wouldn't have to work for it."

Roe laughed and shook his head. "You don't have to worry. And I don't know where you got that from—I'm not dating. I'm looking."

Oh. He'd downloaded one of those dating apps, so...I just figured.

"She's right, though," he said. "I am hot as fuck."

I snorted.

Objectively, I guessed he was right. Even I could say I was drawn to his infectious smiles, but that was where I drew the line. I let the men and women who often flirted with him do the talking for the rest.

"Can I tell you something without you freaking out?"

I lifted my gaze to the rearview again and raised my brows. I wasn't the freaking-out type of person.

He rubbed the back of his neck and smiled unsurely. "I think I might be bi."

What?

As in, he was attracted to both men and women? But he played his straight card at the club just like I did. Had he hooked up with someone there? I shifted in my seat as an unfunny feeling settled in my chest. It felt a little tight. Like it was some worry I couldn't identify properly. No—not Roe. He was straight! He flirted for tips. He fucked women. He'd definitely gotten luckier than me in LA. Every now and then, he'd go home with someone and wake me up with breakfast and a new idea the morning after. I knew he didn't like to stick around the woman's place for long; he always came home early. But still. He spent the night away sometimes. Or he used to. It'd been a while.

I'd only met one woman after Nikki, and it'd been over in two dates.

I cleared my throat, realizing Roe needed me to say something.

"Have you met someone?" I asked carefully.

I reckoned I couldn't blame him for his apprehension. I'd reacted weirdly back when the job offer at the gay club had been on the table. But I'd come around a lot. I could throw flirty smirks men's way too. Gay men didn't automatically make me uncomfortable anymore, and Mom's voice wasn't as loud in my head.

I'd struggled with guilt, at least some, but I knew my mother was in the wrong here. I'd known that for years. I could still hear her hushed lullaby-like chant as she drew her fingers through my hair as a kid. And I hated that part. I hated having those words in my head at all. I didn't even remember all of them— just this nauseating, heavy sensation. And something like... *We keep quiet, we keep quiet, my darling, we keep quiet.* She'd wanted me to forget something I'd seen. Then church had followed. She'd dragged me with her until I'd been old enough to stand up for myself.

Fuck, I didn't wanna think about that. I genuinely feared I'd suppressed something I didn't want to know. Fragments of memories threatened to resurface sometimes, and for some reason, I saw my grandparents on Ma's side. Maybe they'd visited. I didn't know. Screw it. Away with those glimpses.

"...just thoughts. I'm not ready to explore or anything," Roe was saying. "But you're okay with it?"

Fucking *hell*, why would he ask me that? Okay, shit, I knew why. But goddammit. "Jesus Christ, of course I am, Roe. You're my best friend. You—you know how I grew up, but you also know I rejected all that shit, right?"

He hadn't actually met my parents in person, but he'd been around once or twice for a Skype call.

"Yeah, no, I know. I guess I overanalyzed—I mean, with how you were before."

I understood him. "I was a dumb fuck who didn't know better," I replied firmly. "And to be honest, I didn't know how conservative my folks were until I'd been out here a while." I used to just call them traditional, and in a sense, that was true. My old man was fairly liberal when it came to politics, and my ma loved to get involved with helping people in need. But their church was definitely a source of something I was no fan of.

Now, every time I flew back to visit, I could feel it. There was a reason I preferred not to go there for holidays that tended to involve the church. No to Easter, Christmas... Last time, I'd brought Colin out for Fourth of July. Nikki had gone home to visit her parents in Spokane anyway, and my mom had nagged about wanting Colin to see where his daddy had grown up. As if Bear could fucking remember that now. Ma would have to be satisfied with Skype calls until Colin was older. She was more than welcome to visit in the meantime, but I wasn't flying with him again anytime soon. Poor boy had cried his eyes out when the pressure in his ears had become too much.

Roe was visibly relieved, and I could kick myself for being the reason he'd worried.

"As long as you don't get weird or treat me differently, I'm good," he said.

I exhaled a chuckle and shook my head. "Just wait. Next time we do a Tequila Licking, I'm gonna assume you have the hots for me."

That broke the last of the ice, and I was glad to hear him laugh again.

"Dada, bowww!"

"Oh, for—" What did bow *mean*? One of life's biggest mysteries.

CHAPTER 3
2012

March 11 of 2012 would go down in history as a fucking perfect day. We'd just celebrated my twenty-ninth birthday yesterday, we were celebrating Roe's twenty-*fifth* this weekend, Colin was in a great mood, Nikki and I were getting along much better, and, as of now, Roe and I were homeowners.

We had the keys.

One *hell* of a mortgage too.

Greetings, Marina del Rey.

Roe and I parked outside the house and just stared. It was a nice, quiet street—but not far away from the bustle. The Realtor had called it everything from an exclusive bungalow to a hacienda dream. I just called it ours. Mine and Roe's. It was perfect. One story, three bedrooms, a big open kitchen and living room, nice patio, even nicer pool, two and a half baths.

The back was so compact that the pool took up most of the space, but we had a decently sized front yard too. We had fucking lemon trees, man.

"If only this place knew what kinds of plans we have for it," Roe marveled.

Big, big plans.

This was going to be the official Two Condor Chicks Production headquarters in the future. We'd have our podcast studio here, our office, and a place to crash for late nights. A place to volley new ideas and put pins on a map. And yeah, for now, it was also our new home.

"Can you fucking believe this?" I had to ask.

"I can't," he laughed. "I totally fucking can't. We've *made* it, Jake."

We absolutely had.

I was so goddamn happy.

Roe opened the gate and walked through, and I followed. Last time we'd been here, the previous owners hadn't moved out yet, but now there was no trace of them. I glanced at the front lawn, where I could goof off with my boy. The hedge was fairly tall, and I liked that. I liked all the greenery too. The couple who had lived here before had loved to garden, and I was actually looking forward to taking over.

Grandma had sent us seeds as a housewarming gift.

But already, we had plenty to start with. Lemons, figs, limes —I was fairly certain that was a plum tree in the corner. Roses, succulents, lilacs...

The moment we stepped into the house, I could see my future ahead of me. We could actually host barbecue nights for the friends Roe had found us.

The gleaming hardwood floors and the beams in the ceiling were dark against everything else that was a natural white color.

We took off our shoes and walked farther in, where everything opened up. The bedrooms to the right, kitchen to the left, living room straight ahead. Big patio doors that let in plenty of light. The pool was right there.

Roe's party this weekend was gonna have an interesting theme. Two of his cousins and his big brother were coming out to help us move—but mostly to visit, of course—and Nikki and Haley were helping us decorate. Just…I was gonna have to make sure they didn't make plans for the garden. Both the backyard and the front would be my territory.

I could already feel my thumbs turning green.

I slid open the patio door and walked out on the deck, and I took a deep breath.

Complete privacy.

The wooden wall on the other side of the pool had been designed for a vertical garden with several pots and flower beds built into it.

Roe joined me and eyed the future barbecue area next to the pool. The spot was shielded by a pergola of some sort, also made from wood, and it had a canvas sunroof.

"How high up on the list is an Xbox?" he asked. "Before or after patio furniture?"

"Right after a new PlayStation," I replied.

We exchanged a grin.

We could fucking afford both.

"Let's go check out the bedrooms again," I suggested. "You have approximately two days to back out of your offer on who gets the master."

At the showing, he'd said it was obvious I should have it since I'd be sharing my room with Colin every other week. But

64

it wasn't obvious to me. We'd gone into this fifty-fifty, and I was happy to take one of the other two.

"No backing out," he replied. "You take the big one and keep the diaper changes in the en suite bath."

I chuckled. Fair enough.

I reckoned most of my room would be dedicated to Colin anyway. I just needed a bed—and my shit could go into the walk-in closet. And speaking of, we had plenty of those. The hallway leading to the bedrooms had several closets. Perfect for...whatever we might need.

My phone buzzed in my pocket, so I pulled it out and saw my sister's name on the display. "Hey, we just walked into the house."

She was moving soon too. She'd found a studio in Pacific Palisades, which wasn't too far away from here. Girl was officially a Los Angeles resident. And, I guessed, our first official employee.

"Wonderful! Did y'all come up with the themes yet? Nikki and I are heading out to blow up your budget."

I snorted softly and headed for the bedroom where Roe was taking a gander.

"We gotta settle the themes," I reminded him. "The girls are on their way out to shop." I addressed Haley again. "Nikki can decide when it comes to the main bedroom. She knows what Colin likes—but...a *little* bit of neutral won't hurt. He doesn't need cartoon wallpaper."

"We actually have an idea for that," Haley replied. "We'll make it work for both of you, I promise. But I need the colors and somethin' to go on."

Right. It was the one task they'd given us.

Roe shrugged. "I honestly don't care. Blue? Green? Gray?"

"He's helpful," Haley deadpanned.

I chuckled, a little frustrated, and removed my ball cap.

"Okay, uh...you remember Grandma's sun-room? I wouldn't mind something like that for the living room." Basically, a lot of white with darker accents. Grandma liked rugs and pottery, mixing darker shades of red, blue, yellow, and green.

"That's great—lots of plants too, yeah? I know you, big brother."

I smiled. "Right. Go with natural colors for the room I'll be sharin' with Colin, then. And..." I looked to Roe again, and he had nothing. Fine. I could be creative. "Bring a bit of New York to Roe's bedroom."

"Say no more! That's perfect. Talk soon." She ended the call.

Roe smiled at me, and it was a different smile. A little softer. "Bring New York—I like that."

Oh, good.

If Grandma had visited that weekend, Roe and I would've had the best of both worlds in LA. Haley and Grandma from my side, and Roe's brothers on his. I might as well call them brothers rather than cousins, 'cause that was what they were. Not to mention behemoths of men—and at six foot three, I rarely felt short. But every Finlay except Roe had a couple inches on me, and their backgrounds as Marines were a shock to no one either. Kyle was still active, if I got it right, as a helicopter pilot. Greer had been infantry much like me, though as a rifleman instead of assault, and he had a foot out the door of the service. Same went for Francis, Roe's actual brother, who'd recently traded his combat gear for an NYPD uniform.

On the other hand, maybe it was best Grandma wasn't here, because when the going got hot and sweaty, shirts came off, and my grandmother had no filter.

With Def Leppard pouring out of the house, Greer, Kyle, Francis, and I hauled furniture and moving boxes out of the truck. The birthday boy was assembling furniture, and Haley and Nikki...well, they gawked, bossed us around, and took care of Colin.

I glanced behind me as I walked backward into the house. This monster of a desk was going into our studio farthest down the hall. Greer held the other end, and I made sure we didn't walk into anything on the way.

"Dada, go!" Colin hollered. "Hi, Dada!"

I chuckled, out of breath. "Yeah, Daddy's goin'."

Nikki picked the boy up and wasn't subtle in how she eyed Greer up and down. "Let me get you something to drink, Greer."

The fuck was I? Chopped liver?

The man had charm for days and took Nikki's flirting in stride.

Once we'd left the desk in the studio, Greer went back outside, and I intercepted Nikki in the kitchen. Colin was playing with some toys on the floor.

Thankfully, we'd filled the fridge and freezer the other day. I grabbed a bottle of water and decided to catch my breath for a second. And let Nikki in on a secret that wasn't a secret at all. Looks might be deceiving, but...

"You know Greer's gay, right?" I kept my voice down.

"No!" she gasped. "Oh shit. I hope I didn't make him uncomfortable." She pouted for a quick beat. "Why him? He's *so* hot."

Yeah, all right. If you were into ridiculously tall men with well-defined muscles...

Fuck that, I had well-defined muscles too, and I was the tallest man around when the Finlays weren't invading LA.

I frowned to myself, wondering why the fuck I cared.

Nikki cocked a brow at me and smirked knowingly. "Do you need an ego boost?"

"Yeah, maybe a little." I had to be honest.

She laughed softly and came over to me, and she snuck her arms around my middle.

This was nice. A new development between us.

She smiled up at me. "You're the hottest of them all."

Keep going.

My mouth twitched. "Don't lie."

"I'm not." Her green gaze softened, even as her smile morphed into a smirk. "Do you know why we didn't work out, Jake?"

Oh fuck, this was a trap. No longer nice. Abort, abort.

I cleared my throat and squinted. "Uh... I recall somethin' about me not caring enough. Your words."

She pursed her lips. "About *me*. When we were together, everything was *fine*. The food was all right, you chuckled at my jokes, the sex was good, you let me drag you out to clubs... We never fought—you walked out when you thought I was too heated."

I could probably not look more confused. What the hell was wrong with all that?

Her eyes twinkled with humor. "But I've seen you laugh till you had tears in your eyes, Jake. I've heard you groan because the food was so good you didn't know what to do with yourself. I've listened to you talk so animatedly about photography and filmmaking. I've been there when you've reworked your whole schedule to squeeze in another project you're passionate about." She reached up and touched my cheek. "It just wasn't with me. *Roe* gets you that way."

Oh.

I swallowed and furrowed my brow.

"I've listened to your podcast, you know," she murmured.

"Ever since you started doing the live morning shows, I've tuned in on my way to work—and you just can't stop talking to each other. He's unlocked something in you. It's a good look. And I want that for myself with someone."

But was she implying— "That's work, Nikki. We work together. We're passionate about *work*."

She chuckled and pressed a quick kiss to my jaw before stepping back. "If you say so."

I raised my brows. "Uh—you don't get to walk away after sayin' that. What do you mean?"

Did she think there was something else between Roe and me? Fucking ridiculous.

I could honestly say I loved Roe. I thanked my lucky stars every goddamn day he'd run after me into that coffee shop to tell me about his idea for a final project, but that was it. He was my best friend. The brother I'd always wanted. My chosen family.

Nikki sighed, and I didn't like the sympathy in her eyes. Was she *pitying* me or something? What the fuck was going on?

"Do you remember your first reaction when I told you about Derek?"

I didn't know what her best friend had to do with this. He was gay. So what?

"I said I wanted to introduce you to Derek and his boyfriend," she went on, "and you looked downright horrified and said, 'No, that's wrong.' It happened so quickly—and you caught yourself. You changed your answer. You apologized and played it off. You said you were fine with it and wanted to meet them. But something made you react so strongly before you could compose yourself."

Colin smacked into me, wanting up, so I positioned him on my hip while my mind reeled. I shouldn't have fucking come into the kitchen. It had been a trap.

"And don't forget that I've met your parents, Jake."

As if I could. We'd flown out when she'd been pregnant.

"Dada, cuh! Cuh? Cuh, Mama!"

I swallowed uneasily and functioned on autopilot to pour water into Colin's sippy cup, and I gave it to him. Then I flicked Nikki a glance and couldn't help but wonder if she knew something I didn't. Had my mother talked to her when I hadn't been around?

That worried me much more than her delusions about my sexuality.

In fact, that part was laughable. I'd never been attracted to a man.

But my mother was off-limits. I'd been on edge that whole trip.

"We keep quiet, my darling...we keep quiet. That's wrong. So wrong. Shh, just keep quiet, Jake."

"Jake! I need your help!" That was Roe.

Nikki smirked faintly. "Saved by the bell."

Funny, I didn't feel saved. I felt sick.

The light was on in there...

Abandoning my plan to dig a hoodie out of one of the moving boxes, I peered into the room Roe had worked on the most today. Our podcast studio and office. His own bedroom seemed secondary.

No one was in here now, so I trailed over to the window to turn off the lamp—when I noticed the whiteboard on the wall. Roe had already scribbled something on it. Christ, our following on social media. He liked to keep track.

I stood right in front of the whiteboard and stared at the numbers.

A lot of it was Haley's work. She'd become such an integral

part of our business. Every day, she sent us a text about what she needed. What kinds of photos she wanted for Instagram, what sort of message she wanted to put out into the world under our names.

Haley knew strategy. Roe created content. I documented.

"I want you to memorize these numbers, Jake. Two thousand followers on Instagram, three thousand followers on Twitter, twelve thousand likes on our Facebook page—and tomorrow, we start our podcast. This is it, man. Shit's gonna explode from here on out."

To think, that'd been only a few months ago.

Our second season of *Nomads* was taking off. Our podcast had gained local popularity, and we'd gone from weekly, prerecorded episodes to a daily morning chat when people were on their way to work. We had a website. We had a few moving boxes full of merchandise that we offered as give-aways every now and then. Across the country, there were people who had tumblers, T-shirts, ball caps, and pens that read "I'm Off Topic with Roe Finlay and Jake Denver." We had a *brand*. We were getting recognized sometimes when we went out.

And it was just gonna keep growing. Three hundred thousand likes on Facebook was gonna become more. A hundred and fifty thousand followers on Instagram would turn into two hundred and three hundred thousand eventually.

With the third season, we had three major sponsorships waiting for us to showcase their products in our production. That whiteboard was going to be jam-packed with ideas as soon as we went into preproduction.

As if all this wasn't enough, we were working on a couple new projects too. Soon, we'd film the morning show too. Roe wanted us on all platforms. And for the first time ever, we were shooting a nature special in another part of the world. A four-episode miniseries about Norway, Sweden, and Finland. We were off at the end of April.

"There you are."

I glanced over my shoulder and spotted Roe in the doorway. "You okay?"

"Yeah." I cleared my throat and scratched my bicep absently. "Just thinkin' about how far we've come."

He smiled and walked over to me. "Overwhelming, right?"

To put it mildly.

We stood there side by side and looked at the numbers on the board.

Our lives had changed irrevocably, and our futures were fused together. Something that brought me a lot of relief. I couldn't picture a life without Roe by my side anymore. So...I understood why Nikki thought it was more than friendship— because, in a way, it was. I'd been floundering before. Now I had someone to share everything with. Deep down, I didn't give two shits about how many people listened to us in the morning; I just loved that moment for myself. We'd sit at that table and shoot the shit, drink coffee, give a lunch recommendation here and there, discuss an article or two we'd read, and give our listeners a heads-up on what was to come for us.

"I can't fucking wait to see Norway," Roe murmured.

"Me either." We'd started devouring all the information we could find. But my favorite part was probably that it would be just the two of us. Now that *Nomads* was turning into a larger production, I had a feeling I would jump at every opportunity to do something with only him. *The Big North* was a project Ortiz had mentioned sort of in passing; it hadn't been Roe's idea or anything like it. It was 100% a network concept, with a script, and I'd been the one to throw our names in the ring.

We wouldn't be the only filmmakers on the project, though.

Roe and I would cover spring. Three other crews had been chosen for summer, fall, and winter.

With projects like these taking up all my time, I felt confident I could leave my past behind me. I didn't wanna waste another second worrying about suppressed memories or just how much my mother had fucked me up.

"Come on, let's get back to the others." I draped an arm around Roe's shoulders and ushered him out. No longer cold, I skipped the notion of finding a hoodie altogether. We returned to the patio, where the Finlays were winding down after our long day.

We'd had pizza and beer, and then after Nikki, Colin, and Haley had taken off, we'd brought out chips, more alcohol, and cranked up the volume on the music a bit.

"We were just saying you should have a firepit here," Kyle mentioned. "Shouldn't be too complicated to build one."

That was a good idea. "Concrete cylinder block should work."

"That's what I was thinkin'." Greer nodded. "Leave the walls thick enough and make a tabletop of wood or stone."

Sounded perfect to me.

"I'll leave it to my gardener." Roe clapped a hand to my back, and we all chuckled.

"Noooo! Ha-wee, Dada, noo!"

I grinned against his belly and blew raspberries to the sound of Bear's squealing. No sweeter sound in the morning, eh? My boy was all ruckus, sleep lines, and pajamas. Impressive bed head too, kinda like his old man.

There was method to my ball cap collection madness. I didn't fucking have time to fix my hair and shit.

"I don't know if he's yelling for his favorite auntie Haley or he's hungry." My sister knew how to make an entrance. She arrived with coffee and an agenda.

"He's hungry." I smiled and let the boy down on the floor again, and he took off at the speed of light toward Haley. "Mornin'."

"Good morning." She smiled back and handed me the to-go bag from the coffee shop. "And how's my perfect little nephew this morning, huh?" She picked the boy up and smooched his face good and proper. "Let's get you some breakfast. Yeah, you gotta have food in your tummy before we go out on an adventure."

Gah. Had to say I was a little jealous. It was gonna be rough not seeing Colin for three weeks.

I followed Haley out into the kitchen, and she wasted no time while she prepared Colin's oatmeal.

"Okay, so first things first," she said. "You and Roe are doing the food-truck thing tonight, right?"

"Yes, ma'am. I'll get you content for at least seven posts." That one was important to me. My tradition with Roe was alive and well, and we still brought Colin with us to Culver City for frequent food-truck dinners. Haley then spread my work out for various days of posting dinner recs on our Instagram. I liked getting the word out about my favorite food joints.

"Perfect—and you're heading to Vermont right after Finland—"

"That's been changed!" Roe hollered from down the hall.

I looked toward him as he left our studio and hurried toward us.

"We're pushing Vermont to last," he said. "I just got off the phone with Ortiz. We'll come home after Finland, and then we have a week to catch our breath before we do New Mexico."

Oh. Well, I liked that a lot more. Our schedule was gonna

be hectic as it was, first doing this miniseries and then immediately jumping into filming for season three while we were technically still in preproduction. But with a whopping eighteen episodes, we had to take advantage and film whenever we could. A bigger production meant more puzzle pieces to fit together.

"In that case, we only have to plan for three weeks' worth of posting," Haley said. "Roe, don't let Jake forget daily photo updates. I need—"

"M'ha-wee!" Colin yelled.

I pointed to him and eyed my sister. "He's hungry."

She laughed. "Even I caught that. You two go off and do your podcast. I got this. I'll text y'all later."

I chuckled and nodded. "All right. Thanks, hon."

"By the way!" Haley said. "Nikki ain't buying your sneakiness with money, just so you know."

I furrowed my brow. "I know she's not. That's why I'm forcing you to do it for me. You're supposed to call it a job perk."

Did she think I was born yesterday? Nikki had long since stopped accepting money from me, unless it was warranted, of course, but if I occasionally wanted to treat the mother of my child to some nice shit she could do with our son, or on her own, I was gonna try every trick in the book. Now, she was gonna have Colin for three weeks straight, and I figured Nikki and Haley already liked to go to a spa together sometimes, so let me pay for it. Through Haley, obviously.

"That's the crap she's not buying, dork!"

"Not my problem." I washed my hands of the whole thing and made my escape. "See ya tonight!"

Minutes later, Roe and I sat down in the studio—the door was locked to prevent sisters from barging in—and we donned our headphones shortly before seven AM.

The studio had really come together in the last couple of weeks. We shared the desk that took up an entire wall, right in front of the whiteboard, saving the rest of the room for what could be visible on-camera the day we went that route. A round table, comfortable chairs, our equipment, and a custom-made sign on the wall with the name of our podcast.

I unpacked our coffee and—oh, nice. Haley had bought breakfast sandwiches too.

This was why we invested in equipment that filtered out background noise. Nobody wanted to hear a person chew or clear their throat. Although, to be fair, we'd become pros at muting our mics when the situation called for it.

"Good morning, you're Off Topic with Roe Finlay and Jake Denver," Roe said as usual. "I'm Roe, and Jake's absurdly excited to fly our new drone next week. You don't wanna know what that thing cost."

I grinned and took a swig of my coffee.

He wasn't done. "I guess what I can say after working with a filmmaker for a couple years is that they're outrageously expensive and snobby people."

I laughed. "In other words, without me, you'd be looking at Roe's mug through a phone camera. Look at this little critter, folks! Y'all can't see it for the shitty resolution, but I swear it's gorgeous. See ya next week!"

"I'd watch that show," Roe told me, eyes brimming with mirth. "I sound adorable."

"Which I can showcase with better equipment." I smirked when he shrugged, and I decided to move forward. "But Roe is right. We're stoked to be off to Scandinavia tomorrow, and my days of renting drones are over. I'm sure Roe will keep y'all posted on how ridiculous I look trying to maneuver the drone."

"It's my job," Roe replied solemnly. "For those of you who don't know, with this type of drone, you get a headset that looks more like half a helmet. In short, the one in charge of filming sees what the camera attached to the drone sees—and few things are funnier than watching Jake with both feet planted firmly on the ground while he ducks and sways to the movements of wherever the drone is flying."

I shook my head in amusement.

"Like Jake said, I'll keep you posted," Roe went on. "And while we're away, you'll see us primarily on Instagram and Facebook. Off Topic will resume as usual as soon as we're back home."

Okay, so maybe I preferred to work alone with Roe, but damn, the network could be in charge of my travel when-the-fuck-ever. We'd never flown business before, and that was only half of it. When we landed in Bergen two exhausting days later, after three middle-landings, with more luggage than we'd ever traveled with before, everything was taken care of.

Apparently, they didn't have a lot of trucks here like we did in the US, but I kinda liked their alternative more. A man with our names on a sign greeted us as we wheeled three luggage carts out of the airport, and seconds later, we were standing in front of a van. A Mercedes Sprinter fully customized for small film crews. Norway had seen their fair share of documentary filmmakers.

It was fucking incredible. I mean, we'd known they were setting us up with rentals as well as accommodations, but we hadn't expected this. The side of the Sprinter had a ladder, and it only took me one glance to figure out why. Camera mounts were attached to the roof, in case we wanted to climb up there and shoot. And the inside was equipped with secure shelves with straps so that our gear wouldn't slide around. As decided beforehand, two backpacks also waited for us. That was the sponsorship deal. We knew which brands would be highlighted

—and for how long. Backpacks, sleeping bags, sunglasses, a thermos, and, in a few days, two kayaks.

No matter how tired I was, this trip was already flooding me with buzzing energy. Three weeks on the road with Roe, just us and nature. Me and my cameras. Wildlife and mountain ranges.

We got on the road toward our hotel; I drove, and Roe went through our schedule. Here in Norway, we'd meet with three guides. The last one was up north currently tracking a lynx for us. We'd arrived in the middle of mating season.

Given that we'd spent approximately three hours in Oslo and hadn't left the airport, we couldn't say a whole lot about the capital. But Bergen was goddamn stunning. Surrounded by mountains and rain clouds.

"How fast is fifty kilometers an hour?" Roe asked. "I can't get my internet to work."

"I think it's about thirty miles...roughly." I'd done my best to refresh my memory, but the metric system would never come naturally for me. We'd obviously gotten good at it in the Marines; metric measurements were part of NATO standard. Still. It wasn't the easiest.

This, however, was the easiest—no, scratch that. But, at least, the best job in the world.

I breathed in the crisp air and got overwhelmed by the mere sight of our view.

Standing up on the roof of our Sprinter, I tracked a white-tailed eagle through the lens of my camera. I almost had to fucking pinch myself. The mountains here were out of this world. Sharp, majestic granite cliffs shot up from the ground, cradling a river—or fjord—some thousand feet below. *Breathtaking* was an understatement.

Not too far away from here, we had the famous Pulpit Rock, a steep cliffside that rose nearly two thousand feet over the slithering fjord.

Leaving my camera on its stand, I shrugged out of my windbreaker, a little surprised it was so warm in the sun. But we'd read up on the Norwegian climate and how it was milder than what one might expect, due to the Gulf Stream heating the waters. Nevertheless, I had all four seasons right here. Snow-capped mountaintops, flowers in bloom on the ground, warm in the sun, cold as heck in the shade, and with the promise of rain all night.

The colors were just spectacular too. The fjord was so fucking *blue*.

Roe sat in a camping chair behind me, working furiously on his notes. Something I liked to document too. Whoever was going to narrate this series would get a lot of material to work with, because Roe left nothing out. In the two days we'd been here, he'd spoken to countless locals and hikers, and he often had his nose buried in a book in between shooting locations.

I found the eagle in my camera again, and I followed its every move as it soared over the fjord before descending. Knowing what was about to happen, I adjusted my settings and concentrated harder. It was a fairly large specimen, and I guesstimated its wingspan to be about seven feet as it slowed down right before it grazed the surface of the water. A rush of excitement filled me, and I zoomed in on the fish caught in the eagle's talons.

A few days later, we welcomed a night out in the wild. We'd had a cabin the last couple of days, and both Roe and I preferred to pitch a tent with nobody around.

It was difficult not to park my ass in the van and go through footage, presumably as hard as it was for Roe to put down his books and notepads, but we'd become pros. While he pitched the tent next to the Sprinter, I built a fire and prepared our last shooting location for the day.

A classic. Forest and half the tent in the background, darkness had fallen, sausages ready for the fire, one thermos with coffee...

I folded a blanket that we could sit on, and then I got the camera ready.

"What do you want this talk to be about?" I asked.

"I was thinking the camping laws since they're pretty unique to the region," he replied, coming out of the tent.

Good topic. I'd made sure the fire couldn't spread. That would look wonderful on film if we discussed a law we weren't abiding by ourselves.

I shuddered as a harsh wind blew through our campsite, and I huddled closer to the fire and got comfortable. We were farther up north, where snow still covered the ground in some places—not just the mountains.

Roe joined me and double-checked so that the correct brands were visible to the camera. Definitely something to get used to.

"Do you have the hot dog buns?"

"Yeah, right here." I dug out six of them before I stashed the bag behind me. "We're recording, so whenever you're ready."

"Cool." He cleared his throat and ran a hand through his hair. I kept my beanie on. "I hope I don't butcher the pronunciation too much." He practiced the word under his breath. "*Allemannsrett*. I think that's how the guide said it. *Allemannsrett*."

He could be goddamn charming at times. It was impossible not to smile. And get a little protective in a way. He had no reason to be nervous. He was fantastic at this.

While he prepared himself, I stuck two sausages on a stick and angled them into the glow near the edge of the fire.

"You know what—let's eat first," he said. "I can't think of a good approach."

"Okay." I nodded. I had a feeling he was struggling with the tone. We were used to engaging with our viewers through comedy, and this wasn't that type of show. It was supposed to be much more informational.

I kept the camera on, though. We never knew when inspiration would strike, and he might find the right angle in the middle of dinner.

"Would you consider a project in the future that's more about people than nature?" he wondered. "Like, more interview-based and stuff. Maybe about underrepresented cultures or...I don't know," he chuckled, "people who've escaped cults."

I grinned faintly. "Yeah, definitely. Not everything has to be about travel and nature."

By the looks of it, he already had an idea. I'd actually proposed something similar last year, because I knew the investigative journalist in Roe loved to sink his teeth into psychology and trauma. Not that my proposal had had anything to do with trauma. I'd just figured it would've been interesting to interview the people who drove around LA selling food from their hometowns in South America and Asia. I was addicted to small-town stories and local cultures.

"Most of it, though. Let's not get crazy," he responded. "But I read something a while ago that stuck with me. One of the books Greer gave me." He'd shared stories about Greer's love for giving away literature. "It was a psychiatrist's research into indoctrination and deprogramming—everything from conversion therapy to showing a former gang member a better path. The good and the bad of altering behaviors and nature, in short."

That sounded heavy. I furrowed my brow and turned the sausages, then trapped the stick under a rock so I didn't have to hold it.

"There was a very interesting section about soldiers, by the way," he continued. "Like how to get in the right mind-set and prepare for war. Talk about dizzying. I had no idea what they put service members through—or how vital it is. But it comes with consequences, you know? When the soldier comes home, for instance. He's still stuck in war mode, for lack of a better term, while the rest of the family isn't. How alienating that can be."

I nodded slowly, with him so far. I could relate to that part very well.

But back when I'd joined the Marines, I'd welcomed the military doctrines they'd drilled into our skulls. I'd become someone else. I'd perfected my compartmentalization skills.

"What I found even scarier is that sometimes you don't need indoctrination to instill something," he said. "I mean, we've heard stories about religious indoctrination—and what I said, shit like conversion therapy—and cults and whatnot. But if a child is involved, there's a risk of fucking them up with a single opinion."

I side-eyed him and raised a brow.

"Your childhood, for instance," he told me. I cringed internally. Did we have to go there? "You've mentioned your mom in particular being very religious. You never liked the church they're part of. She must've told you things from the bible growing up that you automatically believed in."

I scratched my jaw and peered into the fire. Couldn't he have this conversation with Haley? She was much more vocal about how we'd grown up. Whereas I'd been raised to respect our mother, Haley had rebelled from a younger age. She'd done the right thing and questioned everything.

"If we're gonna discuss my childhood, I'm turnin' off the camera." I jumped to my feet with a resigned grunt and paused the recording. Then I quickly deleted the last video before I returned to my seat. "Of course, when I was little, God was practically a member of the family. He was as real as anyone else." I didn't remember actually doubting the existence of God, and I wasn't sure I did that now either. As my superiors in the service liked to say—there was no atheist in a foxhole. I liked the comfort and the notion of a god, and I wasn't too fussy about the details.

I'd prayed in Afghanistan. I'd prayed when Nikki went into labor. I had friends who rejected the whole notion of religion—a sister too—and I had friends who prayed and went to church. Faith was incredibly personal, and nothing I wanted to ask people about. On the other hand...

"My stance on religion—or the congregation my folks are part of—changed because of how they preached," I explained. "I think I was eleven or twelve when I started getting uncomfortable. It was less God loves all his children and more everyone's going to hell."

I didn't react well to fear. I hated feeling scared, because—

Fuck. My stomach tightened, and an unease spread in my chest.

I scrubbed a hand over my mouth and jaw, remembering very well that one time I'd been so frightened that I'd actually wet my pants. It hadn't been in Afghanistan.

"Do you think they're part of a sect?" Roe asked carefully.

I shook my head. Sect was a strong word. My mother was from Georgia, and my old man was from North Carolina; when they'd moved to Norfolk, they found a church that represented the teachings they'd grown up with. Nuclear family—husband, wife, kids, the American dream. Values they still stood behind. But the world was moving forward, and so was the church. Last

I'd heard, their new youth pastor had a Pride flag bumper sticker affixed to his car. Mom didn't like that one bit.

"Everything I hate about my ma, she got from her own mother," I said. "I'm not typically one to wish misfortune on anyone, but I'm glad that old lady isn't around anymore." She'd died about ten years ago. Not a minute too soon. "She was the kind of person who didn't believe women should vote."

"Jesus," Roe muttered.

"Mm." I had no fond memories of her. Which was a shame, because I'd really loved my grandfather, but every time they visited, Grandma Lucille had to ruin things. Everything was wrong. She'd complained day and night. "Easter was their holiday. That's when they visited us in Norfolk."

Goddammit, Roe had caused the memories to come flooding back now. Same thing every fucking year. Grandma Lucille and Grandpa George came up for the week; she turned our lives into living hell, after which Ma took over. Once they went home again, Ma was so hopped up on Grandma's hatred that she turned into a version of her.

That lasted at least a couple months, until we headed down to Florida to visit Grandma Josephine and Pops over the summer. They'd been the aloe to a burn. That was where I had recovered somewhat.

My grandfathers had died the same year, when I was fourteen.

"We had a lot of tension in the house that made me question things too," I said. "I never really felt the peace and love they preached about at church. My dad thought Ma's side of the family was too extreme, and my mom responded by sucking the life out of the house with silence. She'd never argue—especially not in front of Haley and me—but we'd feel it in the air."

I released a breath, feeling a phantom anxiousness that'd essentially been a part of me growing up.

Roe reached forward to turn the sausages again.

"Haley acted out. I closed myself in," I added.

"I'm not the least surprised to hear that," he murmured.

Heh. Yeah. Maybe. Silence had been easier. Just ride it out.

No, I'd had enough. Time to wrap this up. I cleared my throat and pulled my knees up a bit to rest my arms on them. "Back to your angle...? Of course I was indoctrinated, and many of the things I once believed didn't require any effort on their part. I'm supposed to be able to trust my own parents. If I'm six years old and they tell me something, I believe it."

Eight. I was eight.

I flinched and looked away, only to screw my eyes shut.

"You keep quiet, my darling. Do you hear me? We both keep quiet about this. Shh, my darling. You don't want to go to hell, do you? That's what happens to people like Grandpa. You don't want to be like him, Jake."

"Jake—are you okay?"

"Yeah." I gnashed my teeth and swallowed against a sudden bout of nausea. Holy fuck, it almost made me gag. Her fingers in my hair, her soothing voice—except, there was nothing soothing about what'd happened. I'd been so fucking scared that I'd been shaking. She'd held something. I remembered the stifling heat in the room and the smells billowing upstairs from the kitchen. She'd been in the middle of preparing dinner. She'd ripped...fuck, what *was* it? A magazine? A newspaper? A picture? She'd ripped something from my hands, and she'd squeezed me tightly. The gleam of a knife—that was it. She'd had that fucking knife in her hand when she'd hugged me, and I wasn't sure I could even call it a hug. Just a painfully hard squeeze oozing with desperation and threat, with that damn knife in my face.

"We're never gonna talk about this again, my darling. We keep quiet. You forget what you saw. He's a sick, sick man who

will burn in hell. And you don't want that for yourself. You don't want to burn, do you?"

"I need a minute," I managed to get out and rose to my feet. "We're changin' the topic when I get back."

Fuck.

Fuck, fuck, fuck.

I pressed a fist to my mouth and stalked behind the van, ignoring Roe calling for me, worry evident in his voice. I needed air. I needed to breathe. Twigs broke under my boots, and I planted a hand on a tree as I moved past it. Just a few feet into the woods, and then everything was dark. Deep breaths. The cold air helped at the same time as it drove tiny knives down my throat. My hands prickled and stung, as if they were going numb. My mouth felt dry. My heart pounded furiously. I blinked and had to steady myself against another tree.

I'd kept my promise. I'd never uttered a word to anyone about that day. I'd buried that memory so deep that I still didn't fucking remember what I'd stumbled upon. Why was Grandpa George a bad man? Given...all the circumstances, I didn't have too many options. In fact, I could only think of one thing that would cause such a reaction from my mother, but it felt so damn impossible.

Had my grandfather been gay?

A strangled sound escaped me, and I covered my mouth with my hand again. No, Jesus Christ, that was absurd. Give me a fucking lobotomy—I felt insane for just thinking about him in those terms.

"Please don't go too far, Jake!" I heard Roe holler. "I'm sorry if I said something wrong. I'm so sorry."

"I'm so sorry, Mama."

A sharp pain radiated from my chest, and I collapsed against the tree with a single thought blaring through my skull. *Heart attack, heart attack, heart attack.* My vision blurred and blackened, but maybe I had my eyes closed. I didn't fucking know. I sucked in some air and clutched my chest, paralyzing fear rendering me useless. I was on the ground; I must've slumped down or fallen on my ass. Holy shit, it hurt. I was having a goddamn heart attack, wasn't I? I was gonna die in fucking Norway, in the middle of nowhere, to the memory of my mother holding a knife to my cheek.

Not a knife.

But something sharp. I could feel the edge of...

Deep breaths.

No. It hadn't been the knife. I'd *seen* the knife. Flashes of yellow invaded my brain, and I knew those walls. The guest room. The room in which Ma's folks had stayed when they visited. Why had I been in there? What had I found—

"You forget you ever saw this picture, Jake. You hear me?"

I touched my cheek, feeling something wet—and that edge. The edge of paper, photo paper. A picture. *God*, I didn't wanna remember another fucking thing. I groaned at the out-of-control spin of countless fragments of memories. Until those fragments began coming together. Haley had been nearby. In the next room, crying in her crib. I'd thought she'd been the most boring little sister ever because she didn't wanna grow up and play with me. So I'd run into the guest room, hoping to find Grandpa there. At least he would play cards with me.

That was it. That was why I'd looked through his suitcase on the rocking chair in the corner—to find his cards. The deck with cool trucks on the cards. Instead, I'd found a photo of two men kissing on a beach.

The nausea exploded within me, and before I knew it, I leaned to the side and threw up.

I woke up to the faint smattering of rain hitting the tent.

I blinked drowsily a couple times and shifted slightly, instantly realizing I felt way too comfortable to move. Heavy too. I felt like I weighed a ton.

My mind was blissfully quiet.

I'd laughed and shaken my head when Roe had told me he'd informed his doctor that he had a severe case of anxiety about flying. It'd resulted in a prescription for some sort of sedative, which Roe only wanted to fall asleep easier. And last night, he'd given me one of those pills. Whatever it was, I would give it five stars.

I usually slept on my back, so it felt weird to wake up half on my stomach. But not as weird as the fact that I was sort of draped over Roe.

Christ, what had he buried us under? The inflatable mattress had become a familiar sensation; I slept surprisingly well on it. But the rest... Our clothes. I remembered stumbling into the tent. I remembered stripping down to my thermal wear, then unzipping my sleeping bag to use it as a duvet instead. I'd never enjoyed being confined in a closed sleeping bag. Roe must've done the same at some point, and he hadn't stopped there. Hoodies, tees, and our jackets were strewn on top of the sleeping bags, applying some extra weight that felt weirdly good.

It was frigid outside, so the layers were nice.

I closed my eyes again and hoped Roe's arm wasn't hurting him. I must've used his shoulder as a pillow throughout the night.

I should be alarmed about that.

His chest rose with a deep breath.

I didn't want him to wake up yet, though I understood it would happen soon. Dawn had arrived, and we had a long day of driving ahead of us. But not yet. I needed a few more moments of silence and tranquility. Last night had been the opposite, even after I'd calmed down. I'd had to come up with some bullshit he would believe, because when I'd mentioned suppressed memories, he'd jumped to conclusions and feared sexual or physical abuse. But I'd left it at memories of my parents' religious teachings. The homophobia and whatnot. I was not gonna mention shit about my grandfather.

After that, Roe had forced me to eat half a hot dog and drink a bottle of water, and he'd given me the sedative.

Roe wasn't too inquisitive of a person outside his job; he respected boundaries, so I hoped he wouldn't dig for more information today. I didn't believe he would, to be honest. What I'd admitted was bad enough—and in his ears too. It'd been kind of humbling to hear him curse out my folks last night.

Was that wrong of me? To feel protected in a way? To be comforted?

Maybe that was why I didn't wanna leave this spot now either. It felt too good to be able to lower my guard a bit. The indulgence would end soon anyway. Let me enjoy it while it lasted.

"Go back to sleep," I heard him whisper.

I exhaled and felt his hand brush along my back.

Never in a million years had I anticipated a trip to Scandinavia would wreck me, or at least put a dent in me. On the other hand, it put me back together too. In the northernmost part of Sweden, we were treated to a late-season Northern Lights show, and Roe and I sat on our snowmobiles in the middle of the tundra and just soaked it all up.

I kept my camera running, but this moment was mostly for me. For us.

One day, I wanted to bring my son to this place.

"I don't think I've ever felt smaller," Roe said quietly.

I hummed and took a sip of my hot chocolate.

"Small is my comfort zone," I murmured. I took a deep breath and exhaled, and it looked like the mist mingled with the lights streaking across the night sky. Neon green danced with a deep shade of pink. "It's reassurin' to know I'm insignificant in the grand scheme of things. Less pressure."

Roe was better at handling a life in the limelight. Not that we had too much of it, but I knew it was coming. Our popularity was growing every day. And still, while our phones went off around the clock at home, more offers coming through, more pitches, more responsibilities, more money, more everything, I felt like a fucking condor chick just flapping his wings and hoping for the best.

One of the many reasons I loved these trips. They were literally a break from everything. On location, I had to focus on filming. This was when our business was solely about Roe and me. My footage, his personality.

"Ortiz said we should bring someone else on board," Roe mentioned.

I glanced at him and frowned. That sounded like the opposite of what I wanted.

"You said pressure, and my mind wandered," he clarified. "If we hire someone to run things in the background, you and I can focus on what we do best. More productions."

Oh. Actually, that wasn't a bad idea. Technically, we'd already included Haley. Her insight into PR and marketing had given us a huge boost.

"It might be nice to have a coordinator of some sort," I admitted. "Coordinator slash agent slash manager slash..."

Roe chuckled. "Exactly."

I smiled and nodded. We could do that.

Then I had to change the topic. The light show above us and the fact that we were slowly making our way toward home made this night feel final in a way. We had two days in northern Finland, and then we were off to Helsinki, their capital, to return to the States.

"Thank you, by the way, for...you know. I feel better."

He didn't need me to elaborate. He glanced up at the Lights again. "Don't get uncomfortable now, Jake, but I love you. You're my brother. I'm glad I was there. And I'm sorry you had to go through something like that growing up."

I swallowed hard as a rush of emotions unfurled within me. Sorry, but I *did* get uncomfortable, though that didn't mean his affectionate words weren't welcome. Just unfamiliar. I didn't know how to react to such a statement—or how to be so *close* to someone as I was to Roe. That had never existed in my life before. I'd had friends, countless of them, and none of them had been very difficult to say goodbye to. We'd drifted apart. I'd left the service. I'd moved. I'd graduated. I'd closed one chapter and started a new one.

Roe was different. I wanted him in every chapter of the rest of the book that was my life.

"You're uncomfortable," he chuckled.

I grinned. That was how easily he broke the ice whenever I froze. "Yeah, but I feel the same too."

He smirked. "I know you do. Grandma Josephine gave me some helpful pro-tips, and now I'm fluent in Jake Denver. I cracked the code."

I let out a laugh, feeling so much weight just fall off my shoulders.

After a layover in New York, we landed at LAX late in the afternoon on a sunny Friday, and Roe and I only had one thing on our minds. Get to Culver City with Colin and stuff our faces with comfort food. Then sleep.

Right outside the airport, where people were greeting loved ones and hurriedly filling their cars with luggage, Haley climbed out of my truck with Colin in her arms. Fucking hell, talk about a sight for sore eyes. I knew they'd waited a while. One of our bags had ended up on the wrong carousel.

"Dada, Woe! Dada!"

Roe and I pushed our carts faster, and Haley helped Colin down when she deemed it safe. Then I had my boy tumbling toward me, and I swooped him up the second he was within reach.

"Ahhh, Daddy missed you so fuckin' much." I hugged him tightly and pressed kisses all over his head. He laugh-cried, struggling with his emotions, and swatted at my beard. He wasn't used to that.

"Oh no, Daddy and Uncle Roe turned into cavemen, Colin!" Haley faked a gasp.

"The words you're looking for are *ruggedly hot as fuck*," Roe corrected her with a grin. "Hey, hon."

Haley giggled and hugged Roe. "Hey, scruffy. You can *almost* pull it off."

I smiled against Colin's chubby cheek and kept smooching him. I had no words for how much I'd missed him.

"Almost," Roe scoffed. "Just because I don't ooze Neanderthal sex like Jake doesn't mean I'm not fuckin' smoking."

God.

Haley cracked up hard—a little too hard, if you asked me—but I was too tired to join in. I just shook my head in amusement and nuzzled Colin's neck.

Neanderthal sex, huh?

Well, he was bisexual, so I hoped he was telling the truth. I didn't mind the ego boost. I'd been out of the dating game so long that a man's compliment evidently did the trick.

Once we'd loaded up the luggage and equipment, I had to relinquish my death grip on Colin for a while and take the wheel. We dropped everything off at home first, and then headed north, first to take Haley home to Pacific Palisades. Culver City was next, and if it hadn't been for the mouthwatering smells of the food trucks that greeted us, I would've turned back for home. I was so damn tired at that point, I could probably sleep in the truck.

"Yeah, you're all mine now, little bear." Roe positioned Colin on his hip and got plenty of hugs too. "Damn, I missed you."

I smiled and took a picture of them.

It felt amazing to be home.

We were greeted like we were coming home too. Along the two long rows of food trucks, the majority of the people knew us by name, and everyone wanted to know what we'd been up to. Some of them followed our podcast, others watched our show, and some checked in with us on social media too.

Not to brag, but Roe and I had made at least seven of them sign up for Instagram. Most of them were already on social, of course, but a few of them were like me. They had to be nudged toward new things. But if we gave shout-outs on Insta, we obviously wanted to provide links.

Colin received the royal treatment as well. While Roe and I shared a fucking fantastic burger as our first meal, the guys at Super-Sized Slider gave my boy a Colin Special—mashed potatoes with cut-up sausage and fixings that were easy for him to chew.

I documented everything, from Colin's face covered in mashed potatoes and ketchup, to the people around us. The smoke billowing from the trucks, the blue sky, the hollering between workers slinging ingredients to one another, the man coming down the row with an old-school boom box on his shoulder, the mamas and the papas who sat on the benches while their children and grandchildren worked.

The second meal was grander, and we found a bar table where we could eat in peace. Colin sat on the table and leaned back against my chest as I crammed half a taco into my mouth. Fuck me, shrimp tacos with lime, guacamole—

"Sweet mother of tacos, this is good," Roe groaned with his mouth full.

Colin giggled sleepily, munching on a piece of banana from the Smoothie Sisters' truck.

"We love food, don't we, Bear?" I sucked lime juice and spicy shrimp off my thumb. "What do we do before we eat?"

"Wawr!" He growled and showed his claws.

I grinned and took another bite, adding the growl that made him laugh.

Over the next couple of months, life was fucking perfect. We hired a well-recommended friend of Ortiz's to join our production company. We'd crossed paths with Seth before, so we already knew we had good chemistry. Roe was initially on the fence, but they got along great and, step by step, Seth assumed a much-needed role in our business.

Roe and I could finally step back just a bit from the work we didn't particularly enjoy and focus on what we lived for.

More and more lately, that entailed research for future projects. And, of course, shooting. We wrapped up our third season near the end of July, though we knew we might have to revisit a few places for more flyover footage. Bad weather cost money one way or another, and we chose to go home rather than stay and wait for drone-worthy sunshine.

"Dada!"

"I'm comin', buddy!" I put the lid back on his sippy cup, grabbed the snacks, and returned outside.

Colin waited at the side of the pool, properly impatient—not to mention too fucking cute in his little swim trunks and Iron Maiden tee—while Roe was in the water. We'd determined we had maybe another half hour or so before we had to get the boy into a new diaper. We didn't need a number-two surprise in the pool.

Colin jumped in place and reached for his sippy cup, and he drank noisily as soon as I'd handed it over.

Wait. I felt my forehead crease as I registered the song playing. Roe was our resident DJ, so I tuned out most of the time. But this was a blast from *my* past.

I threw him a look and raised a brow.

He grinned. "I found your old iPod."

What the hell? I looked toward the patio and could barely believe it. He wasn't using the stereo in the living room. He'd hooked up my old docking station to the outdoor speakers we'd installed, and he'd placed it on the patio table.

"I can't believe you like Green Day."

"I grew up with this," I said defensively. Don't talk shit about Green Day. *Dookie* was their heyday. And it sure as fuck beat the music my parents listened to.

Roe laughed. "Oh my God, please tell me you went to shows in black eyeliner."

I rolled my eyes and grabbed Colin's sippy cup before he could toss it on the ground. The boy had zero finesse, and he had no fears either. That was why one of us had to be in the pool at all times when Colin was out here. He just jumped right in. Thankfully, Roe was ready and less than two feet away.

Colin squealed happily and wriggled in Roe's arms, reaching for one of the toys floating around.

I set the cup and the snacks on the side table before I jumped in too.

The water felt damn good in this heat, but I fretted some about Colin's exposure to the sun. He should be good, though. He was pasty white with sunscreen, and he was wearing a tee and trunks.

I swam over to Roe and Colin and felt the top of his head. He refused to wear the little hat Nikki had bought him, so we just had to be careful.

Mesmerized by the water, Colin entertained himself with two rubber penguins and babbled animatedly. All Roe had to do was keep him above the surface.

I pushed my hair back and brushed a hand down my face.

"The image becomes clearer and clearer," Roe mused. "Punk rock was your rebellious phase, wasn't it? Do you play any instruments? Did you sneak out to play in a garage band?"

I chuckled and shook my head. "No garage bands. I learned to play piano and guitar in church, and I never missed a curfew. Sorry to disappoint."

Roe quirked a lopsided smile. "That's still hot. Musicians, man."

That was funny. Interestingly enough, the only man he'd ever mentioned as hot—except for me, partly in jest—was the singer of Maroon 5. It'd sort of caught me off guard since he never spoke about his attraction to men. I didn't know if he'd dated one yet. Last time, he'd said he wasn't ready, but that was a while ago.

"Shouldn't be too hard for you to find one in this town." I could admit, I was digging a little. Sue me. After we'd quit bartending, I just never saw him around men in that type of environment. When we went out, we did that together, with or without friends.

"Yeah, maybe." Roe watched Colin for a beat. "I actually have a date this weekend, but I might cancel."

Oh. Yeah, no, that made sense. I'd grown so accustomed to us ordering pizza and either working or throwing our asses on the couch that I took it for granted. Sometimes we played video games too. He was getting decent at *Call of Duty*.

"Why would you cancel?" I prodded. Was it a dude? Was he gonna go out with another man? Had he already? I didn't know what he did when Nikki and I got together to do something with Colin—or when I worked late with Ortiz.

He shrugged and reached for another rubber toy floating by. He gave it to Colin. "I don't know. I usually go for more assertive women, I guess. She's kinda young too."

So it was a she. That was good. I didn't know why that was good, but it felt better.

"How young?"

"She just graduated from college."

How was that a problem? She was old enough to order a drink at a bar, and Roe was only twenty-five.

I cleared my throat. "I'm sorry to break it to you, buddy, but we won't see any headlines about your age difference."

He snorted softly and gave me a wry look. "Hilarious."

The date was on.

Roe had just left.

It felt weird. I wasn't used to being on my own on a Saturday night. No offense to my son, whom I was in charge of for another couple hours. Nikki had a date too. Actually, it'd started last night, so it must've gone well if they were still together. Either way, I was happy to have Colin an extra day, and I chased him through the house while I waited for him to get tired.

My boy was a runner and a wrestler.

With countless toys scattered across the floor in the living room and the hallway leading to the bedrooms, we ended up somewhere in the middle of it all, with me on my back, rough-housing like pros. I lived for his laughter, the joy in his expression, and how carefree he was. He climbed on top of me as I felt my phone buzz in my pocket, and he growled victoriously and bounced on my stomach.

I *oomph*'d through a chuckle and tickled his belly.

Then he wanted me to chase him again, so he took off.

I might actually fall asleep before he did at this rate.

"Dada, po!" He fell on his butt but got up again with a shout. "Bang!"

My little clown. I sat up too, and I checked my phone.

Dammit. A text from my mother.

Call me, please. We don't talk often anymore.

She had to be getting desperate if she was texting. But I just couldn't maintain the same relationship anymore. It took too much energy to sit there on Skype once a week as she prattled on about life in Norfolk and gushed about how quickly Colin was growing up. I'd become a pro at dodging calls and making up excuses, and once we did sit down over Skype, I kept things brief.

She would have to wait. Colin called out for me again, and I cast a glance toward Roe's bedroom. Hell.

"Not in there, baby." I got to my feet and stalked after him. "We don't go into Uncle Roe's room." Roe must've forgotten to shut his door properly. I found Colin tugging on the nightstand drawer, and I smirked and hurried over to scoop him up. The boy was learning. He knew he could always find a pacifier in my nightstand drawer. "You won't find anythin' in there, Bear. Let's go." I blew a raspberry on his cheek, then bent down to close the drawer—and I just stopped.

What in the name of sex toys. Holy fuck. I slammed the drawer shut and hurried out of the room, making sure to close the door this time.

"Dada, bam-ka-bammm!"

Jesus Christ, that'd been a dildo.

So Roe was into *that*.

CHAPTER 4
2013

"That's good. It was the only missing piece, wasn't it?" I trapped my phone against my shoulder and grabbed the pizza box from the back seat.

"Yeah, we should move on to the next step in a week or two," Seth replied. "Ortiz wants to schedule a roundtable discussion as soon as possible."

"Perfect. You know our schedules, so no need to double-check with us beforehand." I shut the door after snatching up the bags from CVS and Ralph's too, and then I left the driveway. "I gotta say, even though we didn't think this project would be green-lit so fast, I'm hopin' we can go into preproduction ASAP."

"That's the impression I'm getting from the other companies as well. This could be huge."

Even better. I was excited.

Seth and I wrapped up our conversation, and I pocketed my phone before I stepped into the house with my good news. Roe needed some. Poor guy had been sick as a dog all week. But sure, it had turned our mornings into comedy gold on YouTube. With Roe curled up in his chair, duvet wrapped around him, stuffy nose, and a big teacup that read "I woke up like this," our podcast had received a boost because people were weird. Same thing had happened the time I'd had food poisoning and had to dart into the bathroom in the middle of the broadcast.

Sometimes, we missed the days before we filmed the podcast, but at this point, we'd become so used to "showing everything." There was no makeup, no script, no nothing. We just shared an unfiltered hour of our morning with the world, and a crazy number of people enjoyed that.

In the kitchen, I ate a slice of pizza as I rummaged through the bags. More painkillers, more tea, more ice cream, more soup, more cough drops, more ginger ale. It was gonna be a wild weekend at our house.

"Jaaake!" Roe croaked from down the hall. "Is that you?"

"No, it's Santa Claus, buddy!" I gathered some stuff on a tray and heated water in the microwave. Tea, a slice of pizza—his request—and the painkillers that put you to sleep. I fetched the last can of ginger ale from the fridge, too, and restocked with the new ones.

My phone buzzed with a message from my sister.

> Uploaded more Nomads bloopers to your YouTube. Fans are in love. ;)

I huffed a chuckle around a mouthful of pizza.

Not everyone was in love. Roe and I were getting our first

taste of the downside of fame, and some people were just assholes. That type of shit had never fazed me much, but Roe could get heated. Which was why we had surrendered control of our YouTube to Haley. Roe and I had no business reading the comments anymore.

Once everything was ready, I carried the tray to Roe's room, where I found him buried under two duvets.

The floor was littered with tissues, and the curtains were drawn to block the sunlight.

A little bit of sun wouldn't actually kill him. Or some fresh air. Maybe I could get him to eat on the patio tonight.

"How's the patient?" I shifted some shit off to the side of his nightstand so I could set the tray there.

"Dead," he coughed. "Feel sorry for me."

"What's the point if you're already dead? I gotta go out and find a new friend."

He groaned somewhere under the mountain of duvets and pillows. "I will fuckin' haunt you if you replace me that fast."

I smiled and flicked on the light, then sat down on the edge of the bed. "You can rest easy. If you die, I'll get a dog."

He pushed away the thick layers and emerged with an impressive bed head, and he squinted at me.

I grinned. He had his adorable moments, this guy. I could admit that.

Upon seeing the tray on the nightstand, he forced himself up and pushed a pillow between himself and the headboard. He was dead set on trying pizza, supposedly sick of soup and ramen. We'd see if his throat could handle the pepperoni and peppers.

He started with tea, though, and he took his temperature again. In the meantime, I gave him the good news. We'd found our illustrators and graphic designers and animators for our

Travel Back project, and we were good to go. Ortiz would set up a meeting soon.

Roe was pleased. This idea was sort of his baby, and I'd developed it a bit.

No fever either, so that was a relief.

"Can I get you anythin' else?" I asked.

"Yeah." He coughed into his fist and reached for his pizza. "Keep me company. We'll put on a movie or something."

We could do that. I excused myself to get the rest of the pizza from the kitchen—and a Coke—and I made a quick detour to my own room to change from my jeans into basketball shorts. I would just sit on the couch in the living room by myself otherwise, so this worked for me.

Roe made room for me on his bed and turned on the TV. "Have you decided what you wanna do for your thirtieth? I still vote for Vegas, you know."

I'd rather not think about it. "What's wrong with a quiet night in?" I got comfortable next to him and pulled up one of the duvets to rest the pizza box on.

"You can do that when you turn eighty." He shook his head and went to his feel-good show, *Arrested Development*. "Just let me take care of it, Jake. I know exactly how it's gonna go. I'll plan something grand, you will bitch and moan, and then when you get a few drinks in you, you'll have a blast and thank me."

In other words, we were going to Vegas.

"On one condition," I said and took a bite of my slice. "Before we go, I want a nice, chill barbecue here at home with my family. That's Colin, you, Haley, and Nikki. Oh, and I guess your girl."

Shit, I kept forgetting about her.

Roe chuckled through a cough. "Don't worry, Sandra's not comin'. I'm gonna break up with her when she comes back from France."

Finally. Thank fucking *fuck*. They just didn't make any sense whatsoever. Roe wasn't supposed to be "the calm one" in his relationship. And yet... No. The times we'd all gotten together, everything had felt off. Even Nikki and Haley were like, really? Roe was hitching his wagon to someone who could only be described as *bubbly*?

"Oh no, what a shame, Roe. I'm devastated for you."

He side-eyed me and cracked up, only to choke on another round of coughing.

I smirked wryly.

Bless her heart—Sandra was a doll, but no. She belonged with her rich family in Orange County. Or in their "château" in southern France, where they were vacationing.

Roe settled down from his coughing fit, and he promised I would get my family barbecue before we were off to Vegas. Partly because family wasn't allowed in the state of Nevada, aside from him of course. And I was good with that. As much as I loved my sister—and the mother of my kid—I didn't want them near me when I got wasted.

Arrested Development sucked us in after that, and we had the same conversation we always did. Would we forever be the out-of-towners who got a kick out of seeing LA spots we recognized on TV? Much of that show had been filmed in Marina del Rey, the place we now called home, and it never got old to see that lighthouse on-screen. Just the other week, Roe and I had taken Colin for ice cream there.

The answer was yes. Roe would always be the hungry New Yorker who saw glitz and glamour out here. And I would always be the semi-reclusive, semi-Southerner who was a bit wary of all things Hollywood.

"Always the two condor chicks," he said, holding up his pizza slice.

I smiled faintly and bumped it with my own slice. *Cheers*.

All right. It was one thing that Roe fell asleep on my shoulder. A whole other when he pulled a *Jake in Norway* and turned me into his body pillow.

I lowered the volume on the TV as Roe shifted closer and planted his head on my chest. It'd been a bad move for me to get this comfortable in his bed.

Warning bells went off in my head, and I didn't fucking know what to do. How did I get out of here without waking him up? He definitely needed his sleep, and I needed to get as far away from here as possible.

The close proximity forced memories upon me that I wanted to forget. It'd happened once before, a few months ago, around Christmas, when Roe had hugged me really hard after I'd almost been hit by a car. I *hadn't*. Nothing had happened. It'd been a close call. I remembered the sheer panic in Roe's eyes more than the incident itself. Then he'd thrown his arms around me, and I'd been catapulted back in time to when I'd found that picture of Grandpa George and another man.

I stared up at the ceiling and swallowed hard as the anxiety rose within me.

Think of anything but that.

Roe had a birthday coming up too. I had to find him a gift. Nikki was moving to a safer neighborhood soon. She'd gotten a better job. Roe's brothers and sister were talking about visiting this summer. I had photos to edit. *Photos. Photo...*

I clenched my jaw.

In retrospect, it'd been a fairly innocent photo. A light kiss between two fully dressed men standing on a beach.

Every now and then, when I couldn't stop myself, questions piled up. Who had taken the picture? Had that happened before he'd met Grandma Lucille? He couldn't have been too young. I'd been eight years old, and I'd recognized the man as my grandfather instantly. What had it been like back then as a homosexual man? Had he led a double life? Did he die unhappy?

"Mama, look! It's a picture of Grandpa!"

I felt the same warmth now I'd felt all those years ago. I didn't want to remember the smile on my face, but I did. I didn't wanna remember that warm sensation either, because it jammed more questions into my skull. What the fuck had I seen in that photo? How had I interpreted that? I'd been too young to see sexuality and love. Right? I'd been too young to understand.

Then Ma had rushed up the stairs, taken the photo from me... Her face contorted in horror, and the knife...

The warmth had dissipated. My smile had vanished. I'd been wrong to smile at Grandpa kissing another man. So fucking wrong.

I had to get out of here. Hugging Haley was fine, getting a comforting squeeze from Nikki was fine too, and I loved every cuddle Colin gave me, but I couldn't be affectionate with Roe. Soon as that happened, I fell down a rabbit hole of fear, confusion, and sorrow. Because of that warmth. It made me so goddamn angry. My own mother had screwed me up so much that I couldn't enjoy a fucking hug with a man. With my best friend.

Shame washed over me because I did enjoy it. I loved this right here. I loved how close Roe and I were. I loved how important he was to me, and how important I was to him. I loved how Roe brought out so many new feelings in me, which forced me to admit that Nikki had been right about her and me. Things had been *fine* between us. A joke had resulted in a chuckle. The food had been all right. But with Roe... Everything was just so much stronger. Every color, every flavor, every memory, every dumb grin.

I let out a breath and willed myself to relax.

I wasn't doing anything wrong, I wasn't doing anything wrong, I wasn't doing anything wrong.

I'd stood up to my mother countless times. It'd been years since I'd let her control anything where I was concerned. So why the fuck was she in my head now? It was insane.

Roe coughed a little and stirred in his sleep, and he turned away from me, effectively trapping my arm under his head. Then he wrestled with the duvet until it covered us both before his breathing evened out once more.

I gave up the fight for one moment. Carefully turning onto my side, I made sure there was an inch or two between us, and I closed my eyes. I didn't have the energy to feel bad about wanting some closeness.

Since my birthday fell on a Sunday, I was still clinging to twenty-nine when we boarded the plane on Saturday morning. The last day of my twenties. The absolute last. Tomorrow when I woke up, I'd be hungover and old.

I placed my overnight duffel and my garment bag in the overhead compartment, then jammed Roe's little rollaboard in there too. Then we got seated and were promptly served juice or sparkling wine, and I accepted a glass of juice.

Once we were in the air, I'd get something stronger.

Given how tense Roe was, I was gonna need the drinks to keep coming.

"You have a horrible poker face today," I told him. "Just how big is this party gonna be?"

"Heh. Not too big." He shifted in his seat and buckled his

seat belt. "But you're not supposed to know there is a party at all, so quit askin'."

I smirked and scratched my nose. "Roe, if you look like you're about to hurl, I'm gonna ask questions. You okay? Anything I can do?"

Maybe he shouldn't have insisted on throwing me a party. He'd only had two weeks to put something together.

He blew out a breath, and something softened in his expression. Then he linked his arm with mine and patted my hand. "You're a good friend. I'm just nervous about tonight. It has to be perfect."

I flicked a glance at our arms and had to fight the most absurd urge to squeeze his hand. I could do that with Nikki and Haley, not Roe. But Christ, something was wrong with me lately. Ever since he'd been sick, I'd felt myself wanting to move closer. And he didn't make things easy for me. Roe was naturally affectionate, whereas I had compulsive thoughts I couldn't shake. Some people couldn't go out on a balcony without thinking they had to jump. I couldn't jerk off in the shower without picturing Roe with his fucking dildo.

Safe to say, I hadn't gotten off in a long time. I might be traumatized.

"You know just a dinner with you would've been perfect, right?" I wanted to make sure he knew that, despite his haunting me in the shower. "We could find a poker table and get drunk on watered-down cocktails."

He chuckled with a shake of his head and withdrew his arm again. "And sometimes, you say shit like that." He flashed me a smirk. "It's gonna be one hell of a party. We'll leave it at that."

All right. I'd said my piece. I'd given him more than one out.

The party was evidently happening, and the only information I had was the dress code. Word for word, "Justin Timberlake Brings Sexy Back," which I'd had to look up online. Nikki had ended up helping me get a suit tailored, and it was apparently very important to leave the jacket and bring the vest.

Roughly an hour later, we landed in Las Vegas, and Roe couldn't really conceal just how much money he'd spent when we emerged from the airport to find a personal driver with a big-ass SUV about to take us to the Cosmopolitan. We'd been there a few times before, though always on our way back to LA when we were dirty and hadn't shaved in a while after a *Nomads* episode. Las Vegas was the natural pit stop if you'd road-tripped in Arizona, Colorado, and Utah. And we'd stayed at that hotel every time because I loved the view. My camera loved the view too.

"Should we get some lunch on the way?" I asked. "We didn't eat breakfast."

"You just sit there and look pretty. I've got it all covered."

I let out a laugh. Okay, then. I was just gonna sit here and look pretty.

Las Vegas was always a fascinating phenomenon to return to. The glittering hotels shot up from the desert, and suddenly the world was anything but *nature*. This was humankind's work. Marble, shiny metal, fountains, glossy black, swimming pools big enough to get lost in, gold, cabanas, flashing lights, and extravagance. Even I could appreciate a bit of that.

It was like stepping into a fantasy.

Once we arrived at the hotel, it seemed everything had been taken care of already. Roe was greeted by a concierge and an assistant of some sort who handed him the keycards—and some information on the down-low. Not for my ears. Got it.

I had to say, I felt special.

The Cosmopolitan was still the new kid on the block, consisting of two black towers with a thousand rooms in each, and the balcony view was...*chef's kiss*. Perfect view of the Bellagio fountain and beyond.

We took the elevator up—way up—and Roe sent me furtive smirks along the way.

"Do I wanna know how much money you've spent?"

"Hey, I gotta treat my work-husband right." He brushed invisible lint off my shoulder, and I shook my head in amusement. He was in a better mood now. I liked that.

At our floor, I followed him down a long, winding corridor until we reached our room.

It was a familiar sight, and yet not. This room was larger than what we usually reserved. Aside from the usual—the big bedroom with two beds, bathroom with a hot tub, and a generously sized balcony—we had a bigger seating area and bar.

Why couldn't we just stay here?

"I know it's early, but I'm givin' you an A+, buddy. This is fantastic." I gave his shoulder a light squeeze as I passed him to go out on the balcony.

"Hey, none of that—" He halted me with a grip on my arm. "You're marching straight into the bathroom to take a shower, and you'll stay in there for—" He checked his watch, ignoring my surprised face. "Twenty-seven minutes. That oughta get the airplane smell out."

What the fuck? It'd been a one-hour plane ride, and I'd showered a few hours ago.

He smiled sheepishly and let go of my arm. "I need privacy. Don't ask."

I narrowed my eyes. Privacy for what? Would the room be invaded by people when I came out?

"Do I gotta dress up right away?" I pressed.

"Nope. The theme for this next part is *comfort*."

Well, I liked that...

Fine.

"A ridiculously long shower, it is." I nodded firmly and then dug out my toiletry kit from my duffel.

I peered over at my phone on the sink and saw Ma's name on the display again. Not a fucking chance. I'd spoken to her four days ago. I was good for at least a few weeks. Fuck, all this was her fault. She was to blame for my issues with affection and sexuality. She was the reason I overanalyzed a goddamn hug. It was her fault I, for some bizarre reason, forced mental images upon myself when I was just trying to get off like a normal man.

Tightening the towel around my hips, I inspected my jaw in the mirror and decided I didn't need to shave. I'd done that yesterday, and a bit of stubble was a good look on me.

What else could I do? I'd gone to the bathroom, I'd showered, I'd brushed my teeth, I'd trimmed my fucking nails, and I'd used every hygiene product the hotel offered except for the shower cap. I'd even put lotion on, and I had to admit, I wasn't a fan of getting that shit in my chest hair.

"Roe?" I called. "Can I come out now?"

No reply. Wonderful.

I picked up my watch and estimated I'd been in here about twenty minutes.

Seven minutes to go.

Usually the time it took me to rub one out, ironically. Would've been *great* to be able to do that. Alas, I was imagining Roe's ass instead of female asses.

I scratched my eyebrow and sighed.

Maybe I could get laid tonight. If I knew Roe, he'd invited a merry band of coworkers we now called friends. My contact list in my phone had never been longer. And there were some pretty faces in that crowd, definitely.

On the other hand, it was never a good idea to shit where you ate, and I would only be interested in a quick release.

Dating held zero appeal for me. *Quick release, quick release.* I cursed and gripped the edge of the counter, and I screwed my eyes shut and went to my regular fantasy. A rough hold on a pair of hips, my cock pounding in and out of a tight—

"Jake!"

Ass.

I snapped a glare at the door, hearing Roe on the other side. I'd heard a clicking sound too; he'd just been out, hadn't he?

"Are you still in the bathroom?"

I clenched my jaw, beyond sexually frustrated, and straightened up. "Yeah. Spending the last day of my twenties counting the mosaics in the shower."

He laughed. "Sorry. Two more minutes. I'll make it worth it!"

I was sure he would, but I was in a mood now. I couldn't help it. I wasn't a man difficult to please, goddammit. It shouldn't be so damn hard to find a fantasy that stuck. My go-to search words for porn weren't out of the ordinary. I loved a good blow job scene, anal, some bukkake, and the occasional gang bang. Plenty of fodder, and still, my fucked-up issues shoved unwelcome thoughts to the forefront of my brain the second my cock got hard.

I had problems.

Perhaps it was a good thing Roe was flying to Seattle after the weekend. A week apart might do us good. He and Ortiz were gonna sit down with one of the companies we were teaming up with for *Travel Back*, while I stayed here and worked with the animators. There we go. Thinking about work never failed. By next weekend, when Roe was back in town, we'd celebrate his birthday, and my head would be screwed on right again. I just needed a break. That was all. We lived together, worked together, spent most of our spare time together, worked out together. It was a lot.

"Okay, you can come out! Wait—yeah, you can come out."

Finally. I took a deep breath and rolled my shoulders, shaking off all the negativity. Roe had gone through all this trouble to give me a birthday party for the ages; I didn't fucking deserve him.

I tightened my towel again, then walked out of the bathroom, and I came to a halt at the sight of the place. How the *fuck* did this happen? I hadn't heard anything! Other than the front door clicking shut a couple times. Jesus, that sweet guy. I mustered a grin and shook my head. A cluster of black and silver helium-filled balloons swayed next to a table absolutely packed with food.

"Happy 30th, Jake" was printed on the balloons, as well as the napkins and... I chuckled. A stack of party hats. Pizza, a bottle of champagne, sliders, chips and salsa, buffalo wings, cake...

"Am I the best fucker you ever knew or what?"

I glanced at him, only to do a quick double take. "Did you shower?" His hair was damp, and he'd changed into sweatpants.

"I ran down and jumped into the Bellagio fountain," he bullshitted smoothly. "No more questions. Let's get some food."

I was in a fucking daze. But clearly, he had access to another room if he'd showered. I'd file that away for later. I was too hungry and too much in awe to push for answers that didn't really matter.

I joined him closer to the table and draped an arm around his shoulders, and I just stared at the spread in front of us. "Yeah. You're the best fucker I've ever known."

Hands down.

"It gets better. Here." He grabbed a gift box next to the cake, a box I hadn't even noticed. "Happy birthday, old-timer."

I smiled and accepted the little box.

Fuck me, it was a watch. One I'd found too expensive to

buy. Roe liked to poke fun at how I could drop unspeakable amounts on cameras and equipment but got hesitant if a pair of jeans cost more than a hundred bucks. I was still getting used to being fairly well-off, and buying a watch for three grand just wasn't on my radar.

I remembered when I was lucky to make that amount in a month. I'd felt rich.

I could hear Roe reminding me that, "In the world of watches, three grand is nothing."

And I would tell him, "But I don't fuckin' live in the world of watches."

I pulled Roe in for a hug, feeling a little overwhelmed. And it had less to do with the watch and a lot more to do with this world I did live in. The one I was fortunate to share with Monroe Finlay.

"Thank you, buddy." I squeezed him a little harder, stealing another second or two, and felt his hands on my lower back.

"You're welcome. It actually works for me that you're frugal. Makes it a lot easier to find you presents."

I chuckled and pulled back, eager to inspect my new watch. It was fucking beautiful. I had great taste. Simple but classic. Black leather strap, stainless steel case and bezel, pale silver background, with black details.

While I put it on my wrist, Roe filled two plates with food and suggested we eat on the balcony. That worked for me. I smiled at my watch, incredibly happy, and made a mental note to up my game for when Roe turned thirty in a few years.

I grabbed us drinks and followed him outside. The room being soundproofed and blasted with AC made the outside this time of year perfect. It was sunny and about seventy-five degrees, and the city noise from thirty stories below worked better than the sound machine my sister slept with.

"I fucking love Vegas." Roe glanced out over the Strip.

I fucking loved this food. And yeah, Vegas too. I got comfortable on the sofa and didn't waste a second in trying a bit of everything. The chicken wings, superb. A bacon and cheese slider went down right after. Beer, stellar. The champagne could wait. I preferred beer. French fries, several dipping sauces, mozzarella sticks—I was in heaven.

It couldn't have been a more amazing day. It was just Roe and me, vegging out, resting, talking, drinking beer, eating our body weight in food and cake, laughing, sharing memories, only leaving the room for a couple hours to lose some money in the casino and to have dinner. Then we were back on our balcony, discussing our *Travel Back* project. Which made me wonder why I would ever want to spend a week away from him.

We could fight like any other pair of friends, but we solved things fast. The rest—I mean, we were the definition of a well-oiled machine. When we were quiet, the silence was comfortable. When we talked, we lost track of time. He made me laugh like no other, and I knew it was mutual. Roe was an expressive guy. He spoke with his hands and held nothing back. If he was happy, you could tell.

After a late siesta, we woke up on the other side of the Vegas coin. The Strip glittered outside, families had stowed away their kids, a younger crowd flooded the streets, and music from several venues traveled up to the balcony.

It was time to get ready.

Roe was nervous again.

I came in from the balcony and tucked my shirt into my pants. "Quit bein' nervous. It's gonna be fun. No bitching from me, I promise."

He smiled distractedly and fastened his... Huh. Suspenders

were a thing in this day and age? They actually looked good. And much more comfortable than this vest I was about to put on. But Nikki had sworn I looked hot in it—and that my ass was sexy in these pants. That was always nice to hear.

I looked at the rest of my clothes splayed out on my bed and figured I would put on the tie before the vest. Might as well get that over with, because I was bound to wrestle with the damn thing before I got it right.

I popped the collar of my shirt and smoothed the tie around my neck, then closed my eyes and went through the steps I'd learned as a kid. Couldn't do it in front of a mirror—I fucked it up every time I tried.

"So, uh, listen," Roe said, clearing his throat. "I wanted to wait till tomorrow because today's about you, but I kinda need to get something off my chest."

I glanced over at him and furrowed my brow. "I don't care whose day it is. If somethin's on your mind, tell me."

He shot me a quick smile and sat down on the edge of his bed. "Okay. Um..."

I gave up on my tie when I noticed he was struggling to find the words. Completely unlike him, so that worried me a little. Was something wrong? Everything okay with his family? Was it about work?

"It's gonna be complicated between Sandra and me for a while," he admitted. "We had a big fight over the phone yesterday, and I think she could tell I was tryna make my way to the exit, so to speak."

I lifted my brows, having no idea where he was going with this. He was breaking up with her when she got home from France in a week, I was fairly sure. Or maybe it was ten days. I didn't keep track.

"She's pregnant."

What?

I swallowed a sudden burst of nervousness and shock, and I stared at Roe. I knew that look. I'd seen it in the mirror once the nausea had faded three years ago. The apprehension, the worries, the fear, the *excitement*. Roe had reached that stage.

Holy fuck.

Warmth slithered in slowly, as did my own stupid smile. Roe was gonna be a dad. Sweet mother of—how long he'd wanted this.

"You're gonna be a dad, buddy." I grinned widely and hauled him up off the bed and into my arms. "Why the fuck would you wait to tell me? This is incredible."

He exhaled a shaky laugh and squeezed my middle. "I'm a nervous wreck, but I'm happy too."

Of course he was. I knew the feeling very well.

"We'll get some drinks in you soon." I clapped him on the back and eased off. "Christ, I definitely didn't see this coming. Now we have two reasons to celebrate tonight."

Colin wouldn't be that much older either. These two kids would grow up being friends eventually, and nothing made me happier. Three years' difference, give or take a few months—by the time they reached school age, yeah, thick as thieves.

"I guess so." Roe smirked nervously and rubbed the back of his neck. "I'm still dreading the potential drama, though."

Right. He'd mentioned something being complicated. "What's that about? You mean because you were breaking up with her?"

"Well, yeah. I had to do a 180 because she was afraid she'd be raising the baby alone." He was visibly uncomfortable, and it pulled the plug on the celebration for the moment. "I panicked, Jake. The second she said she didn't wanna have an abortion, *but*... I started lying my ass off. I mean, it's one thing to have an abortion if you don't want to become a parent—that's... Whatever, we don't have to go into that." No, it was easy to see he had strong opinions on the matter, and they might have a little some-thing to do with his Catholic upbringing. "But she was talking in terms of me not sticking around. Like, if that were the case, she didn't wanna be a single mom. And that's fine. Fine, I get it. But I want nothing more than to be a dad, so I was like…" A breath gusted out of him, and he slumped down on the bed again and covered his face with his hands.

Oh boy.

What exactly had he said?

"I made a commitment," he confessed, and his hands fell to his sides again. "It wasn't exactly a proposal, but I told her if that's what it takes for her to believe me—to believe I will be there for her—so be it."

Jesus.

Before I even knew it was happening, I was sitting down on the edge of my own bed, zero strength left in my legs. He'd fucking *marry* her? This wasn't the fifties, for chrissakes. Why couldn't they do what Nikki and I were doing? We were acing the co-parenting gig. Sure, it'd been tense and awkward between us for a while, but now we were great friends.

I no longer had to worry about something being missing, like I had when we'd been together. Same old story, the girlfriend at the time said she loved me, and I choked. Thankfully, Nikki hadn't gotten that far with me either, though I sensed that was because she'd known for certain that I hadn't been anywhere near in love. But now? What we had was genuine. We could be happy for each other, we could be a united front for Colin…

"I panicked," Roe repeated.

I coughed and cleared my throat. "I'd say that's a fair assess-ment. How did she react?"

He let out an empty chuckle. "She was over the moon."

I fucking bet.

Goddammit.

Unfortunately, now wasn't the time for me to brood over what this could mean. Roe was clearly distraught, and he'd been there for me so many times. It was my turn to return the favor and lift him up. I could process later.

"Listen—focus on what's important, Roe. You're gonna have a kid." I rose from the bed and pulled him up once more. "We'll worry about the semantics another day. All right?" I nudged up his chin and knocked it gently with my knuckles, kinda like my old man had done when I was little. "When push comes to shove, none of this matters once you get to hold that tiny creature in your arms. You'll look down at your child, and a whole new world will open up." With it, another universe of fears. But we'd save that for the next pep talk.

Roe let out a breath and nodded once. "You're right. I know you're right."

I was always right. Sometimes.

I had my moments.

The first ominous sign was ending up on a higher floor that didn't look like the others. This was for *venues*. This was for the private parties.

The second sign was when we arrived at a door guarded by two guys who'd missed their calling as linebackers. Roe had hired *security* for this fucking party. At that point, I knew he was gonna take "grand" and run with it. Far. Beyond the horizon. And the music. It was pumping from the inside.

"Happy birthday, bro."

His grin was the last thing I saw before I was ushered into what could only be described as a small VIP nightclub. Absolutely packed with people. Undoubtedly over a hundred guests.

I didn't know that many people.

I exhaled a laugh, both thrilled and fucking scared.

It was Roe's version of a perfect party, but that was okay. More than okay. He knew how I functioned. Gimme a few drinks and I was good to go.

"Happy birthday, Jake!"

"It's Jake!"

"Jake, over here!"

"Happy birthday, man!"

Fucking hell, it was dizzying already. Purple lights flashed in the darkness with a white static light that made everyone move like robots. Balloons covered the ceiling. Oh, I knew those two. Gina and Neil. Seth was here with his girl. I nodded and grinned at them as Roe guided me over to Sean, Robyn, Thierry, Cub, and Michael. Wait—I was pretty sure I just saw someone famous. Who *were* these people? Industry folk, no doubt. Everyone was dressed to the nines and partying it up. The DJ— I recognized him too.

I shook more hands and bumped more fists than I could count, and thank fuck, I had a drink in my hand within a minute.

"We're not Hollywood, Roe!" I yelled over the music.

He grinned up at me and leaned close. "You sure about that? Look around you, Jake. Did you think five million weekly listeners weren't gonna leave a mark?"

But...

I was just a documentary filmmaker.

I took a big gulp of my drink and watched a woman walk by with a flirty wave. Roe spoke in my ear. She was a famous Instagrammer or influencer. A couple LA-famous comedians were here too. Some up-and-coming actors. The thrifty little fucker that was my best friend had turned this into a networking opportunity, and half the booze flowing had been sponsored in return for exposure. He and Haley had apparently worked on this all week.

"This is the place to be tonight!" Roe finished. "Your sister's words. Tomorrow, everyone will be talking about Jake Denver's thirtieth."

I shook my head, in a complete daze, and replied the only way I knew how. "Get me drunk, you dumb genius."

"Interesting nickname! I'm on it. Let's go. I know someone who's dying to see you again."

What? Who?

Roe took the lead through the dancing crowd, which I swore was growing for every minute that passed, until we ended up at the bar. And I could only smile like an idiot when I saw who was on the other side.

Juan. Of-fucking-course.

He rounded the bar and threw his arms around my neck, and I chuckled and hugged him back.

"Don't think I'm gonna let you forget about me, Jake! Happy birthday!"

"Thank you. You're kinda unforgettable."

He eased back and lit up. "That's what I like to hear. Did you see the screens? I swear I've Instagrammed each image! My God." He fanned himself, but I was just confused.

Roe smirked slyly and linked his arm with mine. "I'll show you! You can blame Haley for providing the footage, but this is my production! I put it all together and edited it!"

Okay, noted.

As Roe's first lady, Lady Gaga, blared from the speakers, some wild remix of "Just Dance," we arrived at the wall nearest the terrace, and I blinked and did a double take as four flat-screens showed an all-too familiar face. My own.

The year "2010" flashed by, and in the background was a

black-and-white photo of me taken up in Big Sur. "Jake meets Roe, and nothing was ever the same." Jesus Christ, he'd put together a slideshow, hadn't he? But he couldn't blame Haley for that photo. Roe had taken it. He'd taken the next few too, and same went for the ones that followed for "2011." Pictures of me, all black-and-white. "Two Condor Chicks Production is born." When I was adjusting the settings on my camera, when I was eating, when I was smirking at Roe, when I was mid-laugh... 2012... Nikki had taken a photo of Roe and me; we were lit in that one, grinning like fools. "Jake gets nominated for his first award, and it wasn't for how sexy he is."

I laughed and draped an arm around Roe's shoulders. I couldn't fucking believe he'd done all this.

2013 was a heartwarming series of photos. Roe and me with Colin in Culver City, Haley and me after a couple drinks, one with Roe, me, and Nikki—my family, in short. They were my family.

And the year had only just begun.

I finished my drink, then saw the images flash again—and...it started over.

1983.

"Jacob Casper Denver is born in Norfolk, Virginia. Future brother, high-school heartthrob, Marine, combat photographer, documentary filmmaker, father, podcaster, YouTuber, and the better half of Roe Finlay and Jake Denver..."

I swallowed hard, and the pounding music faded into the background.

Suddenly, my chest felt tight. Just seeing all those things listed like that did something to me—even more so because it was Roe who'd organized it all. He saw my achievements in a light I wasn't sure I did myself.

These were the photos Haley had provided. The slideshow sped up to gloss over my youngest years, up until I graduated high school, then when I became a Marine.

I side-eyed Roe. He was watching the slides with an easy grin on his face.

At some point, I'd started preferring to observe the world through the lens of my camera. I'd completely forgotten that some people would see me too. No matter how hard I tried to blend into the background, I'd earned a leading role in a select few people's lives—and I never wanted to take that for granted.

It was ironic. On the night Roe shone a bright spotlight on me, I saw him better.

I couldn't fucking lose him.

In the light of the slideshow, his eyelashes seemed longer. His dimples more pronounced. He had faint freckles too. His eyes...captivatingly beautiful. And his grin, always so infectious.

If he married his girlfriend, chances were he'd move out. No husband about to become a father stayed with his buddy and roommate. I saw no alternative outcome. He was gonna pass the leading role over to his wife and child. Nothing else made sense. They'd live in their own house.

I glanced back at the screen as 2010 reappeared.

"Jake meets Roe, and nothing was ever the same."

I swallowed again, picturing the year to come. Pages that were still unwritten.

2014. *"Jake gets demoted to secondary character."*

I needed a new drink.

Alcohol was good. Alcohol was great. But Roe was my drug. Wrapped up in a thick vodka haze, I was sober enough to know I was getting possessive but drunk enough not to give a flying fuck. When Seth and his girlfriend, Dominique—and her friend Alexis or Alexa—told me it was time to hit the dance floor, I went willingly because Roe was eager to join.

I downed my drink and disappeared into the crowd. Gina and Gabe from Little GNG Productions came with us, and with a smirky look and a silent question from Gina, I found my partner. As long as I stayed close to Roe, I was good to play along. And Gina was safe. Happily married to Neil, who didn't like to dance.

I spun her into my arms and gave her cheek a smooch at the same time as Roe pulled Alexis-Alexa close next to us.

We were packed like sardines, moving to the quick, semi-seductive R&B beat, and Gina made it easy for me. She was a good dancer and lost herself in the music, her back to my chest, and I kept a loose grip on her hips and peered down. Tight leather pants hugging the curves of her ass and thighs—and *nothing*. I *liked* her. I liked working with her on *Travel Back*. She was fun and incredibly talented. But I was more focused on Roe's hands on Alexis-Alexa's hips than on Gina's ass.

I shook my head quickly, my vision feeling more unfocused. Fuck, definitely drunk. A liquid heat flowed through me, and I sent a skyward glance toward the blurry balloons on the ceiling and let out a labored breath.

It was hot and dizzying, and I lasted about six songs before I was too thirsty to stick around.

Roe suggested the roped-off area in the eastern corner next to the terrace and told Gina and me to go ahead. He'd get us drinks.

"No detours!" I told him. He was mine tonight. I needed to get my fill if he was on his way out of my life, if only partly. Call me sick—that was how I felt.

He threw me a lopsided grin, and I detected surprise and confusion in his eyes, but he nodded in understanding. He probably guessed I wanted him as a social barrier, even though I always lost that desire once I started seeing two of everyone.

Gina and I squeezed through the crowd, and we picked up

Neil and a few others on the way. Jason, Kai, and Sonny worked with us on and off on *Nomads,* a team of brilliant editors and digital artists.

"Awesome party, Jake!" Jason hollered.

"It's all Roe!" I called back. Gina grabbed my hand, still in a dancing mood, and I grinned and twirled her around as a guard let us through to the private area. She smiled drunkenly and shimmied her hips to the beat, then danced over to her husband.

I glanced around me, instantly noticing how the volume dropped a bit. The nook was by no means cut off from the rest of the club, but Vegas knew how sound worked. At least here, we could carry on a conversation without shouting. The ceiling was lower, and the two large sofas with accompanying chairs were boxed in on three sides.

I aimed for the corner of the couch farthest in, and Gina and Neil followed. But then Kai sat down on the other end, while Jason and Sonny went for the chairs, and that posed a juvenile problem for me. One that proved how fucking insane I was. It was gonna be a tight fit for Roe, but I wanted him next to me.

It was my birthday party, wasn't it? That's right. So I decided.

Work was what we all had in common, meaning it didn't take a genius to figure out we dove for shop talk. Jason and Kai were curious about our *Travel Back* show, and Gina was happy to divulge the concept.

"Basically, Jake and Roe will travel the world and take the viewer back in time to various events," she said excitedly. "For instance, they're going to Eastern Europe and Italy for the first episode to talk about the plague and how it spread across Europe. And in the *fourth* episode, I think they're visiting Mexico to cover the rise and fall of the Aztecs. It's gonna be fucking amazing!"

Her obvious excitement rubbed off on me, and I sat forward

a bit to see Kai easier. "We're gonna draw parallels between then and now too—like, you'll see what it looked like back then and what's there nowadays. Part history, part travel and tourism."

"Sounds like a great project," Sonny noted. "I'm guessin' it'll be a fairly large production."

I inclined my head. "Aside from Roe's and my crew, we'll have a topography team on-site for aerials and so on. We'll need a fuck-ton of footage for the animators to work with."

"I was gonna say—must be a whole lot of studio reconstructing," Jason said.

Yeah, that was gonna be the biggest job of all. Hence why so many were involved.

I spotted a familiar figure emerging from the mayhem in the main club area, and Roe wasn't alone. He had Juan with him too. I'd learned Juan was in charge of the bartending staff tonight but wasn't mixing any drinks himself—which was good. I wanted him here as a buddy, not staff.

They didn't arrive empty-handed. Both men were carrying large trays filled with alcohol, mixers, and snacks, and I was ready to make room for Roe.

"Anyone interested in getting smashed?" Juan beamed.

"You know it." I sat forward some more and jerked my chin at Roe. *Get over here.*

He smirked faintly and eyed the others on the couch. "Excuse me, everyone!" He rounded the table and—Jesus Christ, he pulled the most drunken stunt and tumbled down on top of us, his head landing on my lap.

"Fuckin' idiot," I laughed.

"Oh my God, Roe!" Gina laughed too, startled.

Roe smiled, pleased as punch, and pretended to sleep.

Not exactly what I'd had in mind.

Roe opened his eyes again and blinked up at me. "Remind me not to close my eyes again. The world's spinnin' too fast."

I chuckled and helped him up, and he scrambled closer to me. Wait, was he—yup, he planted his fucking ass on my lap and leaned back against the armrest. Even when Kai opted to sit on the couch across from us instead.

"Consider this my throne for the night!" Roe clapped his hands and rubbed them together, then zeroed in on the booze on the table.

Gina shook her head in amusement and cuddled up with her husband a couple feet away. Roe would fit next to me now, but he didn't move.

He bobbed his head to the music and started mixing us some cocktails, prompting the others to join in. Nobody turned down free booze. In the meantime, Juan introduced himself as the man who'd discovered Jake and Roe, to which Roe and I cracked up.

"So how did you meet?" Gina asked, puzzled.

I chuckled and scratched my nose. "Roe and I bartended at the gay club Juan works at."

"I'm part owner now!" Juan informed us proudly.

No shit? Roe gave me a glass just in time, so I raised it to Juan. "Congratulations are in order. That's cool—"

"Fuck me, this is my song." Roe interrupted.

I snorted. Every song he liked was his song. But maybe this Katy Perry tune wasn't gonna work for me, 'cause Roe couldn't sit still. I didn't know who'd once taught him to dance, but he had a knack for it. And he wasn't afraid to move seductively.

Dude.

He was sucked into a conversation with Juan and Gina about a Katy Perry show they'd both been to—*like, oh my God, you were there too?*—and all I could focus on was Roe's ass. Shit.

I took a gulp of my drink, tasting vodka and tonic and lemon and fucking hell, quit moving.

I cleared my throat and heard a voice in the back of my mind, but I couldn't grasp the words. Just...it was a warning. This wasn't normal. I should gently, politely shift him off my lap.

I didn't do that.

Because it felt good.

Too good.

Mother of fuck.

I chugged my drink and told Roe to make me another.

Then I loosened my tie and tried to distract myself. I eased into Neil and Sonny's discussion about permits for location shoots, and I sympathized with Sonny and his crew because they were being forced to move a project out of state to save money. It was all politics. Some states begged filmmakers to come; others made us jump through hoops.

"No shop talk!" Roe handed me my drink and tried to scowl at me.

Too fucking cute.

"You're too drunk to look mad." I smirked lazily and sipped my drink. Fucking amazing—he knew how to mix 'em. "Besides, you've said I'm too hot to be pissy with."

"*That* you remember," he deadpanned. "But when I want you to empty the dishwasher, I gotta remind you twenty fuckin' times."

He was so goddamn funny when he spoke with his hands. The Brooklyn guy came out in full force when he'd had a few.

"I empty that thing way more than you do," I chuckled.

"Because I don't like it." He emphasized every word and grinned, satisfied, when I laughed.

He started moving to the music again, but I got stuck on the worst thought. Were our days of bitching about cleaning almost over? Roe was *lazy* around the house. He was the creator. The one who stirred up a mess in the kitchen and then walked away. The one who hauled out video games and snacks, then got a call and forgot about the rest. But I didn't mind. Without his initiative, I'd lead a boring life.

I emptied another drink and got caught in a dizzy spell. He couldn't move, dammit. He couldn't leave me. I wasn't ready to share him.

Fuck.

I wedged a hand between the armrest and his lower back, steadying him a bit. If he wanted to shimmy to the music and lip-sync with Gina, he'd have to stick to my thighs. I couldn't have him moving over my cock.

My cock was untrustworthy these days.

And Roe's little ass wasn't bad to look at.

If I was gonna be honest and all. But I had no clue how he could fit a dildo in there.

"Jake! Roe!"

I furrowed my brow and struggled to fix my stare on...Juan. He was holding up—of fucking course. Shot glasses and a bottle of tequila.

"For old times' sake," he insisted. "I bet Gina wants to know what a Tequila Licking is."

Roe groaned a laugh.

"Uh, *yeah*." She did. "Do I want one?"

"With your man—absofuckinglutely." Roe nodded. "Jake and I will show you."

Oh, would we?

It'd been a while...

"It's a not-so-creative body shot," I drawled. "Instead of taking the shot off your partner's body, you lick the salt off him instead. Roe's hardly the inventor."

"Will you fuckin'... Why you gotta be like that?" He gave me a bleary-eyed glare, then refocused on pouring the shots.

Gina looked on with mirth in her eyes.

"I'll be a good boy now," I promised.

"Oh no, we prefer bad Jake." Juan winked at me.

Bad Jake made bad choices.

Bad Jake had fewer limits.

Bad Jake was really beginning to love having Roe on his lap.

I rubbed his lower back slowly, and he held up the salt. I tilted my neck, exposing it for him, and he poured some salt across my skin. I was handed the lime wedge next, so I bit into the peel. Then he said cheers to everyone and threw back the tequila.

He grimaced and shuddered like he always did, before he dipped down and licked the length of my neck.

Fuuuck.

I squeezed his thigh automatically and shivered, and he finished by sinking his teeth into the lime wedge, causing juice to trickle down my chin.

Once he backed off, I swallowed the lime flavor and wiped a hand over my chin.

"That never fucking fails!" Juan fanned himself.

I grinned crookedly.

Gina was quick to give her hubby some foreplay for later tonight, and I was honestly relieved I was off the hook. I couldn't concentrate worth a damn, the club was spinning, and I felt too hot. Shots at this point would send me to the nearest bathroom within the hour.

I might have to switch to beer.

Roe draped an arm around me and dipped down to speak in my ear. "You havin' a good time?"

I nodded and shifted underneath him, needing a better

angle. Fuck yeah, that was it. I didn't care anymore. Put the pressure on my cock. My thighs were going numb.

"You drunk?"

I let out a laugh and nodded sluggishly. "Plastered."

Was I touching him too much? I wasn't sure. I couldn't stop rubbing the top of his ass, right below his belt—same with his thigh. If others noticed, it had to look weird. But one voice I couldn't get to shut the fuck up was the one telling me Roe was leaving me. He was gonna move out and get married and start a family with fucking Sandra.

"No more booze for you," he said, his lips grazing my ear. I felt another shudder roll through me, but I was too hot to enjoy it. I needed air. My shirt was practically sticking to my skin, and I was done wearing a tie.

"Let's go outside for a minute," I slurred.

He nodded.

How I got off the couch was a fucking mystery, and thankfully Roe handled the talking. He told the others we'd be back in a while, and then we made our way out of the private area, which was when I realized I really had to take a leak. I managed to convey that to Roe, and we changed direction. We had to get to the other side of the club. He grabbed my hand and did the dumbest thing. He started leading me across the dance floor.

Holy fuck, I could barely walk properly. People dancing, everything moving, my mind spinning madly, the music pumping, the *heat*... It was stifling.

It didn't help that the DJ had switched to playing hookup music. At three AM, it was time for people to find the person they'd share a bed with. The provocative beat, heavy and slow, rocked through me, and I looked down and reacted too slowly. When I bumped into Roe, I got assaulted by too many images of moving bodies. But they were naked this time. That's what this was. A playground for getting laid. Grinding, sliding, kissing, and rubbing. Roe squeezed my hand harder, and I placed a hand along his side.

We were almost there.

We got through, and Roe's body heat disappeared momentarily when he hurried to the bar and talked to someone. I leaned against a wall and scrubbed my hands over my face. Jesus Christ, I couldn't breathe in here.

"Jake!" Roe was back. He nudged me toward the bathrooms, and he produced a key.

Damn. We just walked past the two long lines until we ended up in a private bathroom with way too bright lights.

"Fuck." I squinted and stumbled over to the urinal, and I undid my belt and pants.

"We're headin' back downstairs," I heard him say. I was too busy groaning because it felt so damn good to relieve myself. He found that funny. "Maybe we overdid it tonight."

I shook my head and planted a hand on the wall. "No." Tonight had been perfect—and I wasn't ready for it to be over. In our room, I'd have no reason to be so close to him, and I still needed that. I needed my hands on him. "We're not leavin' yet. I'll switch to beer."

He let out a laugh. "Baby, you should switch to water and cake. Get some of that fat to soak up the alcohol."

Baby.

I raked my teeth over my bottom lip and tucked myself back into my pants. Then I went to wash my hands and wondered if I'd already gone too far tonight. If there was a way to turn back. Or... Fuck, I didn't know what I meant. But I wanted to push further. I wanted to cross lines. Keep him close. Touch him. Feel him. Have him pressed against me. He was mine tonight, right? My birthday.

I took a deep breath and let it out slowly.

"Hey, if you insist we stay a while longer, at least come down with me first," Roe said. "I need to charge my phone."

"All right." It was a plan. We'd come back up here, and I could make more bad choices.

We headed out again, and Roe returned the key before we aimed for the exit.

The last couple of drinks I'd had were coursing through my system, pushing me between soaring freedom and limitless urges. I stopped caring about the world spinning too fast; I wasn't feeling *bad*. No nausea, no headache. That was all that mattered.

The music echoed in my head almost as loudly as in the club once we ended up in the quiet corridor.

Before long, we were in the elevator going down, and I looked up at the mirrored ceiling and loosened my tie further. I was done with that thing.

"You look hella fuckin' good tonight."

I dropped my gaze and found him watching me with a faint smile.

Roe wasn't shy about saying that kinda stuff to me, and he probably didn't know that it meant something. I, of course, never said anything in return, because I was the dumbass with dumb sexuality issues. But they weren't holding me back right now.

"So do you."

He quirked a cute grin and walked out of the elevator. "That's how I know Jake Denver is shitfaced. Come on."

Hold up. My reflexes didn't work like that. I had to pull myself out of the elevator, and Roe was a dick. He laughed at me—then saved me, because he was a nice dick. He stepped under my arm and let me lean against him, which was much better. I was close to him again.

"I'm findin' my words," I told him. "To thank you, I mean.

For tonight, for being my buddy, my Roe. You know it ain't easy for me—but whenever you say somethin', I wanna say, yeah, me too."

My Roe.

He smiled up at me. "I know that, Jake. You have your own way of expressing yourself."

Okay, great, but I still wanted to say it, and now I finally could.

"My point is, I can't picture my life without you anymore." I fell against the wall as Roe stopped to open the door to our room. Hell, I thought it was farther down the hallway. "I think you and I should take our kids back to Norway one day—show them where our first major production took place. And your thirtieth birthday is mine. You did all this for me—so that's the deal. When you turn thirty, you're mine."

Fuck, I had to stop saying that.

Mine.

My Roe. Mine.

Whatever—he was amused. Fine. I meant every word.

I followed him inside and was thankful when he only flicked on a couple of the lamps. No bright lights. Cozy and nice.

I removed my tie and threw it somewhere.

"Whatever you want, baby," he joked.

Baby.

I scratched my forehead, and it felt like a sealed box was rattling in some remote corner of my brain. Trying to tell me something. I didn't know. But as he headed into the bathroom, I went after him and had to say something.

"You've changed a little since you told me you're bi," I said.

He glanced at me, confused, maybe wondering why the fuck I had followed him into the bathroom when he was clearly trying to take a piss. But why? Did I care? No. We were beyond that. I could talk while he took a leak. The toilet was in its own little room in the bathroom, so I leaned against the doorframe and waited. And talked.

"You're more, I don't know—you're sweet," I told him. "You pay me a lot of compliments, and I'm stupid to never say anythin' back. But that's beside the point. You don't share much about your datin' life. I don't know if you've met a dude. You only mention girlfriends."

"Boy, did I unlock Pandora's box when I poured liquor into you tonight," he mused.

I grinned and lifted my brows. I wanted answers. Had he met a guy? Had he kissed another man? Gotten fucked? Had they played with that dildo together? I had to know. The women were bad enough. Now I had to bat away dudes too? I couldn't catch a fucking break.

He stifled a belch and flushed the toilet. "I haven't done shit with a guy."

That was good. Real good. I liked that answer. I could relax.

Still feeling too hot, I unbuttoned my vest and took it off. "Isn't it quiet here? My ears are ringing. We should put on some music."

He cracked up and shook his head at me. "You're just all over the place, aren't you?"

I shrugged and walked out, wanting to find music. There should be music on the TV.

Roe helped me once he was done in the bathroom. I could count on him. He was a good guy.

I smiled and threw an arm around him. "You're a good guy, Roe. The best." This music was perfect too, because it was the same we'd heard upstairs. "Louder. I miss the club feeling. Did you charge your phone yet?"

"We'll head back up there as soon as you pass out," he promised, removing his tie.

I nodded. "Good."

It shouldn't take too long to charge his phone. Scratching my neck, I eyed the bar and decided to make a drink. Shit—I grimaced at the feel of my neck. Sticky and probably salty. I walked over to the bar and undid my shirt a little.

I kicked off my shoes and almost stumbled when I tugged off my socks too.

"You sure you wanna do that, Jake?"

"What? You want tonic or cranberry with your vodka?" I didn't wanna waste my perfect buzz. The dizziness had gone down a bit, and now I just wanted to chill. Listen to music, drink, be with my Roe. I wanted to laugh at his crude jokes and hitch my future to his dimpled grins.

"You know what?" Roe hurried over to me and stole the vodka bottle from me. "What you need is a refreshing shower and some food. It'll make you ready for round two upstairs."

A shower wasn't a horrible idea. I was sweaty and covered in salt and lime juice. At least on my neck.

"Can you order room service?" I asked. "I want ice with my vodka."

"I'll—yeah, definitely. Let's get you into the shower. And while you freshen up, I'll mix your drink and order up food. How's that?"

Perfect, that's what it was.

He ushered me into the bathroom again, a little too fast for my abilities, so I steadied myself against the sink. And he bent over to pick up my vest.

That ass.

Jesus.

I swallowed against the dryness in my throat and watched him straighten up. He draped the vest over the edge of the bathtub, and it was such an insignificant sight, but I wanted to find my camera and take a photo of him.

I loved taking photos of Roe.

"You're supposed to take your clothes off and hop in the shower," he reminded me.

"I'm supposed to do a lot of things." Yet, all I could do was stare. As if...if I stared a bit longer, I'd understand something that remained out of reach, beyond my comprehension.

He gave me a strange look, maybe because I wasn't making much sense—who knew—and he dismissed it. He came over to me and finished unbuttoning my shirt, then slid it down my shoulders.

Closer, closer, closer.

I'd never paid attention to those freckles. I liked them. You only saw them up close, turning them into a secret for people who had no business being mere inches away from him.

I liked his hands on me too.

And his eyes. I hadn't noticed they were more green than blue.

"You're staring, dude." He put up a front with that smirk, and no amount of alcohol could prevent me from seeing through it.

I dropped my gaze to his lips and wondered...

My shirt fell to the floor, and he was right there, about to take a step back.

We couldn't have that. It was too soon for him to leave.

"My pants aren't gonna come off on their own." I gripped the edge of the sink behind me, making it clear I wouldn't make this easy for him.

A flash of uncertainty flickered in his eyes, but I knew Roe Finlay. He recovered quickly. He landed on his feet and faced challenges head on.

Closer, closer.

He'd started this. He'd fucked with my head, unknowingly, for months. Maybe longer.

"Are you bein' obstinate on purpose?" He narrowed his eyes at me.

No *baby* this time?

Another kind of heat made its way through me, fueled by a boost of assertiveness. I liked this look on him. Just a tad out of place. Not quite knowing how to read me. What to do next. So I reached out and tugged him closer, and I leaned in and grazed my nose along the shell of his ear.

"It's better you undo my pants for me."

He sucked in a breath and froze, and I took advantage. I brought his hands to my belt and helped him get cracking. The belt came off while I inhaled deeply through my nose, and then his fingers trembled and worked my zipper.

"You're not gonna remember this tomorrow," he rasped.

I prayed I fucking would.

I wasn't sure I'd ever felt anything like this. Hell, I wasn't sure I *knew* what I felt, only that it was all-consuming and over-whelmingly powerful. Forceful. My entire being buzzed with a desire I'd never experienced before, from my core to the surface of my skin.

He tugged the zipper down, and his fingertips brushed over my boxer briefs. My cock.

I exhaled. "Keep going." I nuzzled his neck, my mouth watering. Remembering I had fucking hands of my own, I reached out and slid them up his chest.

His breaths came out faster.

He pushed down my pants till they fell off and pooled at my feet.

"Almost there," I murmured. I slid off his suspenders, then began unbuttoning his shirt too. At the same time, I ghosted my lips along his jaw and waited for him. *Show me something new, Roe.* He wanted me. He was always *extra*...when I was drunk. Because he was indulging. He was banking on me forgetting his terms of endearment when I woke up the following morning.

"You rat fucking bastard," he whispered. Last thing he said before he surrendered and tilted his face toward mine. Our lips met, and I cupped his face in my hands. A violent shiver tore down my spine, and I deepened the kiss right away.

He moaned as I swept my tongue into his mouth. He fell against me and kissed me back hard, passionately. Lust exploded inside me, and my chest expanded with a quick breath and the urge to take whatever I could.

He was mine tonight.

This was *right*.

The second I dropped my hands, he locked his arms around my neck, and I lost my patience. Feeling his body against mine was so foreign and yet felt so goddamn wonderful. With zero finesse, I got rid of his shirt and undid his pants, and he took over after that until there was nothing left on either of us.

Not *quite* ready to look down, I steered him toward the shower and kissed him again. He took the hint and blindly reached out to open the shower door. It was a big shower. Plenty of room. He turned on the water overhead, and I backed him up against the wall.

He gasped, and fuck, so did I. Whether I looked or not, it was impossible to miss the sensation of my cock pressing against his. My mind started swimming all over again, a few silent cries of panic easily silenced by my hunger.

"Wait," he panted. "Slow down—Jake, wait."

He put his hands on my chest and gave me no choice but to comply. But the kissing—we had to get back to that. I marveled at the feel of his slight stubble under my fingertips, the shape of his jaw, and how sexy the contrasts between soft and sharp were. He was so undoubtedly masculine, and somehow that made the gentler sides of him all the more appealing.

In a way, it was Roe who had taught me that men could be more than...how I'd been raised.

"We're not gonna take this too far." He gave me a nudge, and I took a step back, ending up right under the water. It was set on that annoying rain setting by default. I'd cursed it out earlier. "Close your eyes."

I wasn't sure that was a good idea, but I did as told and waited to feel unsteady again.

Roe touched my chest, and I realized he'd used the body wash.

"You had your hands on me a lot tonight," he murmured.

Goose bumps spread across my skin, and I let out a long breath as his hands roamed my upper body. That was what I wanted. Touching. His hands on me. My hands on him...

"Yeah."

"Here." He grabbed my hands and poured something—okay, body wash. Then guided my hands to his body, and I got with the program. If he wanted us to wash each other, so be it. We could do that, as long as we kept touching.

I mirrored his movements. A heavy, seductive exhaustion washed over me, and I wasn't sure I could open my eyes again. I didn't get dizzy as I'd expected. It just felt good. Even more so when he rubbed my shoulders, my arms, my chest, down to my abs.

I rested my forehead to his and slipped my hands to his back. His breathing hitched when I dropped lower, and fuck it, sorry for being so impatient, but I had to feel him. I captured his mouth in an unhurried kiss and squeezed his ass cheeks. Two perfect handfuls, equal parts soft and firm.

The rain setting wasn't so annoying anymore. Since it didn't wash away the suds effectively, my hands glided freely wherever I wanted them, and a rush of possessiveness and lust took hold of me as I slid my middle finger between his cheeks. He whimpered into the lazy kiss and snaked his tongue around mine.

Right there—I rubbed his tight little opening, and the fantasies just smacked into me. So maybe it wasn't a faceless woman I pounded my cock into. Maybe it was Roe's delectable little ass. *Fuck me.* Sue me, I'd always been an ass man.

"*Fuck.*" I groaned at the feel of his fingers on my cock. We deepened the kiss, and he soaped me up as much as he fucking teased me. "You tortured me upstairs. Sittin' on me like that."

"Yeah? I couldn't help it. Everyone wanted a piece of you tonight."

And he wanted me all to himself?

I shaped my fingers along his jaw and tightened my hold, and then I finally allowed myself to push harder. The tip of my middle finger disappeared into his ass, and it was as intoxicating as I knew it would be. Jesus, he was tight. He squirmed against me and pushed out his ass with a breathless moan, and I buried my finger knuckle-deep.

"You like that?"

He sucked in a breath and nodded quickly.

"Do you play with yourself like this?" I could picture him in the shower at home, a thought that made me harder. "Finger-fuck yourself and jerk off? Or do you use something else?"

Even in my drunken state, I didn't wanna put him on the spot about the dildo I'd accidentally seen.

"Just—fuck. We gotta stop. Or I don't know. It feels so good," he groaned. "No, wait. I gotta think."

Thinking wasn't good. Thinking led to slowing shit down.

But fine. I withdrew my finger and stroked him lightly between his ass cheeks instead. It seemed I couldn't keep my hands off him.

I didn't know how long we stayed in the shower, but by the time Roe turned off the water, I knew my cock wasn't gonna go down without a release. He'd said we weren't gonna take this too far, and I didn't know what he meant. What was too far? We weren't done, were we?

I managed to pry my eyes open, and I blinked drowsily. My mind screamed at me. *Get him under you.* Fuck, the mere thought. Trapping him under me on a bed, where he couldn't escape. I imagined his blunt fingernails digging into my shoulder blades.

He walked around me and opened the door. "We need fresh air. I'm not sober enough to think for the both of us."

Fuck being sober. Yeah, probably not the healthiest mind-set —I realized that—but alcohol killed my panic and silenced voices from my past. Now...when I looked at Roe, I saw someone I couldn't get enough of on a whole new level. I craved him like fucking air.

He tossed me one of the bathrobes, and I put it on.

We weren't done.

Back in the room, Roe stopped at the table that'd been filled with food earlier, and he grabbed whatever was edible from the abandoned leftovers. Cake, cold pizza, chips, and bread. Last but not least, a couple Cokes from the bar fridge. Then he headed out onto the balcony, which...seemed cold. Vegas was warm enough by day, but at night? In March?

Whatever.

I eyed the top of the fridge where he'd just stood to find us sodas, and something else caught my interest. Las Vegas to the rescue. It wasn't a hotel in this town unless the room had some- thing for one-nighters and lovers. I grabbed the tin box and opened it, ignoring the condom, ignoring the weird little vibrator thing, and fished out the packet of lube.

I pocketed it and headed outside.

Definitely chilly.

Joining him on the sofa, I looked out through the glass

railing to where Las Vegas was slowly but surely wrapping up another wild night. Cars honked, people shouted, drunks were on their way back to their hotels.

I played nice long enough to take a swig of the Coke and eat a forkful of cake, but that was where I drew the line. When Roe gave me an apprehensive look, his posture radiating tension, I coaxed out his surrender. I leaned over and kissed him; it didn't require more than that. He fell against me, and we went from zero to sixty in a second. I moaned as he climbed on top of me, and I was quick to dig underneath his robe and palm his ass.

"We should stop," he groaned into the kiss.

"Do you *want* to stop?"

"No."

Then we weren't fucking stopping.

We made out like teenagers, with the distinct difference that I'd never once fooled around with a woman with so much lust raging within me. It fueled my every move and made me need more.

I opened his robe fully and kissed his chest. He shuddered and tipped his head back. As I flicked my tongue over his nipple, I played with his ass and brushed my fingertips over his asshole over and over, and he held me in place by weaving his fingers into my hair.

I just couldn't get past how sexy his ass was. I had to finger it with the lube. I wanted to see how many digits I could push inside.

He dipped down and kissed my neck. "Let me take care of you."

He could do whatever the fuck he wanted.

He eased me back against the cushions, and I scrubbed a hand over my mouth. It was the first time I saw him properly. Even though it was dark out here, the sight of him would be etched in my brain forever. That swimmer's body, his cut abs, his...his cock. I swallowed dryly. He trimmed more than I did. His balls looked so smooth.

I wanted to—

Wait, where was he going?

He slid down my body until he was kneeling between my legs, and he opened my robe some more.

Fuck me.

"This is what I get off to in the shower, by the way." He wrapped his fingers around my cock and pressed an open-mouthed kiss to the head. "Among other things."

I shivered and cupped his cheek.

No words could describe the moment he sucked me into his mouth. Slowly, inch by inch, soaking me with his soft tongue, enveloping me in warmth. And he didn't break eye contact either. It was *my* cock he was sucking, *me* he was staring at so hungrily, *me* he desired.

Fuck, he looked good with my cock in his mouth.

One shudder set off another, and I couldn't stop staring. I slipped my fingers into his hair and controlled his pace, and when he moaned, I felt the vibrations around my cock.

So warm and wet and tight... "Keep goin' like that." I barely recognized my own voice. "Fuck." Part of me wanted to shut my eyes and just savor the sensations, especially when he cupped my balls in his hand too.

The harder he sucked me, the more self-control I lost. All of a sudden, I had to have everything at once, so I ordered him to get up on the sofa. I needed his ass within reach, and I showed him the lube and said I wanted to finger-fuck him. To which his eyes widened, and then he was hurrying.

He leaned up and kissed me hard, swiftly, and got on all fours next to me.

"Get back to sucking my cock, Roe."

I tore the corner off the packet and drizzled some lube onto my fingers, and just as he sucked me in again—and gagged a little, which felt too good to admit—I got my fingers back where they belonged. I caressed the sensitive crease between his cheeks and spread the lube around, making sure my digits were properly coated.

"That's it," I groaned.

With his head blocking my view of what he was doing, I could lean back and just feel. I teased him a bit, going back and forth, back and forth, all the way down to his balls. They *were* smooth and tight. Full. Christ, I hadn't expected that to turn me on so much.

Feeling bolder, I traced my fingers along his cock too, before I rubbed lube into his skin and gave him a few strokes. He whimpered at that, and I told him to stroke himself. I didn't mean to be selfish, but I wanted to play with his ass.

My lubed-up middle finger sank into him with ease, and the angle let me feel more of him than in the shower.

We found an instinctual rhythm of me thrusting slightly into his mouth and him pushing back against my finger, and that was it. This was where I wanted to freeze time and get lost in the moment.

"This tight little ass of yours...is drivin' me fuckin' crazy." I pulled out and rubbed the opening with two fingers, then slowly inserted both.

He moaned around my cock, and I twisted my wrist and fucked him gently, stroking and rubbing his inner walls. My mouth watered. Now probably wasn't the time to see if he'd be interested in a tongue-fucking... Few people were, in my experience. It was just a fantasy of mine. I'd never come close to actually going through with it.

Roe's lust-filled sounds grew louder, another thing that chipped away at my self-restraint. He'd become bolder too. He sucked more of me, harder and faster, and he jerked himself at the same pace. When he gagged, he stayed there until he could breathe through his nose again.

My chest fell and rose more rapidly. I wasn't ready for it to be over, but the pleasure intensified so quickly, and I couldn't hold back worth a damn.

Three fingers buried in Roe's ass got him going, and his reactions pushed me so close to the edge that my body's urges took over completely. I fucked his mouth and held his head in place all while I worked his ass with my fingers hard enough for him to jostle forward with each thrust.

I heard him choke, and for a hot second, I worried I'd pushed him too hard. But then I felt hot splashes landing on my thigh, and I realized he was coming. Holy fuck. *Holy fuck, holy fuck, holy fuck.* It felt like something detonated within me or like something snapped in half, and it became my undoing. Feverish and dizzy with dark desire, I let the pleasure rush through me as I started coming too.

I couldn't even warn him, it happened so fast.

The waves knocked me over mentally, and I didn't really know where I ended up. I wasn't breathing; that much was clear. I had my eyes screwed shut too. I came and came, until I had to force air into my burning lungs. My thigh cramped uncomfortably, but I managed to stretch my leg out.

"Oh my God," he croaked. "Holy fuck."

I was panting. Jesus Christ. I swallowed against the dryness in my throat and couldn't fucking stop trembling. His forehead landed on my thigh, hopefully not where he'd come, and I carefully withdrew my fingers from him.

He shuddered too.

Seconds ticked by, and I let out a long breath. I had no words. Fucking hell, this was what sex was all about. This was the mythical, mind-numbing pleasure. I had no strength left in my body.

"Are you alive?"

I drew in a deep breath. "Unclear."

He let out a weak chuckle and lifted his head, then sat back and pulled his robe shut.

"That was..."

"Yeah." I'd been missing out.

Fuck, even my mind was empty. I had nothing.

Except...when I threw him a drowsy look, it didn't take more than a second to realize he was already way ahead. He was wondering what happened next, and I had the answer for that.

Despite that I was nowhere near stable, I dragged myself up and off the sofa with a grunt that belonged to someone decades older than me. I shrugged out of my robe, ignoring the cold, and wiped off his come. Then I grabbed his hand and nodded toward the door.

I couldn't speak, but I could write the end of this chapter by showing him.

After ushering him inside, I turned off all the lights, shut off the TV, and dragged him with me to bed. Under the same duvet, on the same pillow, I fused myself to him, his back to my chest, and I buried my face against his neck.

No maintaining a distance this time. I took the comfort and the affection I'd wanted when he'd been sick. I held him to me, rubbed his chest, and felt his heart slow down, breath by breath.

My head had never felt so heavy. Nor my eyelids.

Goddamn noise.

I pulled the duvet higher up and wished that the incessant ringing would fucking stop.

"Hello?"

No. No hellos. Only goodbyes. Let me sleep.

Oh God, the *headache*. That was it. I wasn't moving another inch. No moving whatsoever.

"Yeah, no, of course—right. Yeah, no worries at all. We'll be down soon."

Nope. I wasn't going anywhere. I'd evidently inhaled an entire bar last night, so I was gonna stay here.

"Shit. Jake, wake up. I got us a late checkout, but we managed to sleep through that too. Our flight's in two hours."

I groaned in sheer agony. Too. Much. Information. At. Once. Where *were* we? Right, Vegas. Birthday party. Slideshow on flat-screens. Cake. Food. All the booze. God, so much booze.

I was thirty now.

Thirty hurt.

"Buddy, I'm serious. We gotta go."

"Jesus Christ!" I bitched. I pushed away the duvet and sat up, and fucking kill me now. "*Ow*." Oh, my poor head. It hurt so much my eyes actually welled up. Wait, was I naked? *Why* was I naked?

I squinted over at Roe just as he stepped into a pair of jeans, and the sight of his bare ass shot a whole bunch of images—fuck, no, *memories*...into my skull. Oh, Jesus fucking Christ. Him sitting on my lap in the club, the touching, going...into the bathroom? I...what? No. Yes. First upstairs at the club, then down here...

We showered together.

We hooked up.

He sucked me off on the balcony.

I fingered the fuck out of his ass.

Oh God. Oh hell.

"Jake," he reminded me impatiently. "I gotta run downstairs and settle the bill. Can you meet me in the lobby?"

"Uh...yeah." I nodded and scrubbed my hands over my face. "Give me—give me two minutes."

Oh my God.

I didn't know what was the most unforgettable—what we'd done or how hardcore I'd gotten off on it. On him. On the two of us together.

Roe was gone in seconds, after throwing on a T-shirt and stuffing the rest of his shit into his bag.

I groaned and rubbed at my temples. What had we done? What was running through his mind? What would happen now? We couldn't fuck up our friendship. I needed that more than air.

Panic rose quickly within me, as did nausea, and my to-do list wrote itself. I rushed into the bathroom and threw up, causing my head to hurt even more. Kill me, kill me, kill me. I was never drinking again—a shitty lie I'd told myself so many times. So, fine. I wasn't gonna go there. But one thing was clear. I wasn't drinking for a while. Because it was all coming back to me. How I'd reasoned with myself last night. How I'd justified hooking up with my best friend because I was fucking hammered. And when I was three sheets to the wind, I didn't hear my mother condemn my actions.

"We're never gonna talk about this again, my darling. We keep quiet. You forget what you saw. He's a sick, sick man who will burn in hell. And you don't want that for yourself. You don't want to burn, do you?"

"I'm so sorry, Mama."

I pulled myself up and pushed through. I splashed cold water on my face, I brushed my teeth, and I chased down two painkillers with more water.

Get through the day. Go home.

I knew my mother was wrong. She was dead wrong. I refused to let her bigotry get to me. But this was a *lot*. Roe and I hadn't merely shared a hesitant kiss and then stayed up all night to talk about it. Maybe that was a thing? Maybe it *should* be? Instead, we'd gotten so drunk that... Whatever. We'd gone far.

I couldn't take the headache. At this rate, I'd throw up in the cab too.

I went through the motions and got dressed in a hurry—jeans, tee, ball cap, definitely my shades. The light from outside was killing me. Then I grabbed my belongings, stuffed them into my duffel, and walked out.

I was fairly certain I'd forgotten the garment bag and the tie, but fuck it. I'd packed the suit, my camera that I'd barely used, and my essentials. I patted my pockets to make sure—yeah, wallet, phone, keys.

I checked my watch in the elevator, and it took me a second to get used to the new sight. The watch Roe had given me.

Deep breaths.

We had to be okay.

I...I wasn't gay, was I? But...last night hadn't been a random fluke. It'd been a drunken awakening, emphasis on awakening. Also emphasis on drunken.

Was it possible to acknowledge you'd made a huge fucking mistake while not regretting a damn thing?

Maybe I did regret it but hadn't come that far in my processing yet. God, I needed to sleep away the whole fucking day.

What happened in Las Vegas stayed in Las Vegas?

Un-fucking-likely.

The ride to the airport was quiet. I was nursing my headache with a complimentary coffee from the hotel, and Roe was nervously checking the time. Once we arrived at the airport, getting through security was all I could handle. Too many people talking too loudly, walking too fast—and fucking honestly, sir, you didn't know you couldn't get through security with a case of beer? Back of the line, moron.

Roe and I finally made it to the other side, and we reached our gate with a few minutes to spare. They'd just started boarding the last group.

"I legit wanna cry," I muttered.

"I feel ya," he sighed. "Did you take painkillers?"

I nodded and closed my eyes for a moment. "We're not doin' shit today, are we? Other than resting, ordering pizza, and inhaling coffee."

"Not a damn thing except that." He cleared his throat and nudged me forward a step. "You, uh...you have to tell me if you want space or—"

I looked at him sharply, which hurt, for the record, but come the fuck on. "Roe, I don't know what the hell happened to us last night, but don't do that. Don't pull away."

Judging by his instant relief, he needed to hear that. "Got it. No pulling away. We'll, um, talk when we get home?"

I nodded again. It was a plan.

It was our turn to board soon enough, and we found our seats in business while Roe checked his phone. I didn't have the energy for that shit. Besides, Roe updated me whether I wanted him to or not. Haley had texted him several times, apparently. The party had created a slight buzz back in LA, and "everyone," meaning *some*, wanted to talk about Jake Denver.

"Uh-huh." I tucked my shades into the neckline of my tee, pulled down my ball cap over my eyes, and folded my arms over my chest. "Wake me up when we land."

Roe chuckled tiredly. "No, I'll leave your ass here."

Let's not discuss asses right now. I was thoroughly confused as it was.

A walk through LAX undid the progress I'd made by sleeping on the plane, and now the headache was back in full force times two. I wanted to cry again. My head hadn't hurt this much since...hell, probably infantry training at Camp Geiger; I'd sustained a concussion during an exercise. But at least they'd given me the good painkillers.

Where were those now?

I got in the cab and rested my bag on my lap, and I just prayed traffic wasn't too horrible. We didn't live far from here, so fingers crossed, we'd be home ASAP.

Roe's restless knee-tapping and fidgeting didn't help, though. I scowled tiredly at his legs as he gave the driver our address.

"Why're you bouncin' around like Colin tryna prove he's not tired?" I asked.

He huffed out a breath and scrubbed his hands over his face, the tapping slowing down. "I made the mistake of catching up on my messages on the plane."

I remembered. Had I missed—

"I saved Sandra for last," he said. "Now I wanna throw my phone in the ocean."

Oh.

Sandra—why did her name leave a bad taste in my mouth? It felt like my brain was trying to jog a memory for me, but any type of jogging right now hurt too much.

"She's comin' home soon, right?" I scratched the side of my neck. Something about a breakup that wasn't happening anymore. No, wait. It was gonna be *complicated* for a while. Because...because...because...

"Earlier than expected, too," Roe confirmed. "She'll meet

me in Seattle on Tuesday morning so we can 'talk about our situation.'" He made air quotes and a face.

What situa—

Oh *hell*. My eyes widened as everything came back to me in a painful rush. They were having a kid! Fucking Christ, how had I forgotten that? Roe was gonna be a dad, a thought that instantly filled me with happiness for him. Except for the Sandra part. I wasn't a fan of their situation being complicated at all. Because...because... Shit, because Roe had promised commitment.

"You're not actually gonna marry her, are you?" I kinda just blurted that out.

He sucked his teeth and looked out the window. "I hope not, but she left me a bunch of messages about how relieved she is. How relieved her *dad* is. He thinks it's the only right thing. If we're having a child, Sandra and I should be married."

Jesus. I'd never met Sandra's old man, but I knew of him, of course. He was a big name in pro athlete management. Football players and basketball players had made Thomas Stevens a multimillionaire.

The rest of the ride home was quiet, and I just couldn't wrap my head around the fact that Roe might be a married man soon. He didn't even love the woman. He'd been moments away from breaking up with her when she'd divulged she was pregnant. What fucking decade had we traveled back to?

I gave Roe some space when we got home. His issues were far more pressing than mine, so I just told him I was here when or if he wanted to talk. I took a shower and crashed for a few hours on the couch. Every now and then, I woke up to hear Roe rummaging through the house. He was packing for his work trip and, knowing him, preparing mentally for the meetings he and Ortiz would have with the others involved in the project from the Northwest. It probably gave Roe a break from the shit with Sandra. Work had a way of offering us both solace.

I used work as an escape too. Rather than analyzing last night's events that I wasn't ready to deal with, I dozed on and off to a documentary on limestone. Later this year, Roe and I were going to Slovenia for one of the episodes, and we had a lot of research to do. The cave system we were visiting told a tale of how Europe had taken shape hundreds of thousands of years ago, and we already had an impressive list of historians and geologists we'd be interviewing.

Freaking limestone.

I yawned and stretched out my legs atop the coffee table.

"Roe," I called. "You want me to order pizza soon?"

I could eat. My head wasn't killing me anymore, and water and Coke weren't cutting it enough. Pizza would be the perfect birthday dinner. Grease and salty goodness.

Roe emerged from his room down the hall—or maybe the studio, I didn't know—and scratched his head. He seemed to be on a mission, and he positioned himself in front of the TV and stared at me.

Pizza wasn't a tough choice. It was a *yes now* or *yes later*.

"You're not gay," he told me.

I felt my eyebrows fly up.

"Correct," I replied automatically.

We weren't gonna discuss pizza, were we?

He nodded once, firmly. "That's what I needed to hear. You can order pizza." He started to leave, his posture and behavior so stiff that it set off a warning within me.

"Hey, hold up." I removed my feet from the table and sat forward. Something was definitely wrong, and I didn't wanna say anything that might be misconstrued. "How about you let me in on the war you're fightin' in your head, bud." It wasn't a question. Ready or not, we had to talk.

Roe sighed and retraced his steps to the TV, and he tossed me a weary look. "I'm kinda freaking out, Jake. For almost two years, I hoped against hope that—" He shook his head quickly and started over. "I gotta get my shit together in forty-eight hours, and I don't even know how to begin to process what happened between us last night. I heard you talking in your sleep."

Okay, slow down, slow down. Hoped against hope for what? And I sleep talked?

He came over and sat down on the coffee table in front of me, and right then and there, I practically felt his exhaustion. He'd been running himself ragged mentally all day, hadn't he?

I was a dick. I should've been there for him. With the marriage bullshit and a kid on the way...I could only imagine what he was going through.

"You said you couldn't lose me," he admitted. "You were mumbling—like, shortly after you fell asleep this morning. You couldn't lose being the leading role or something in my life."

Oh fuck. Embarrassment crashed into me and settled heavily in my gut. I did remember my fears from yesterday. My possessiveness. My worries. How I hadn't been able to let him out of my sight.

I cleared my throat and shifted in my seat, and I... It was wrong to say I didn't know how to respond; it was more a matter of not wanting to be so vulnerable. Shit—to fucking sleep talk like that? How goddamn mortifying. And dumb. Of course I was gonna lose that position. Of course I was. I hated it, and it wasn't about him having a kid. It was my irrational jealousy toward a woman I barely tolerated. Which I didn't wanna admit to Roe, who might actually marry her.

"I'm..." Fuck. I rubbed my forehead and groaned internally.

I had to give him something. The gist of the truth. To be fair, he'd already stated it. I just had to confirm he was in the right ballpark. "I'm protective of what we have, I guess you can say," I said, feeling awkward as fuck. "I know we said living in this house was gonna be temporary—just until we could afford our own homes..." This house was supposed to be the headquarters for our production company. We both loved the idea of our workplace having a homey feel to it. More relaxing. "But it's gonna suck if you move out. Which I obviously understand you will if you stay with Sandra. Y'all can't exactly raise a family in your bedroom."

Roe nodded minutely and stared at me as if he were trying to work out a math problem. "So you got spooked. That's why we crossed the line last night."

Oh, I—no. That...that was going a bit too far. While my stupid fears definitely played a part, my... Jesus Christ, I could barely conjure the word in my head. *Attraction.* My attraction. My attraction to *Roe*—or whatever it was—was a separate issue altogether. Possibly triggered by those fears or...I didn't fucking know. I wasn't ready to think about it. I wasn't...I wasn't gay. Gay was a simple definition, right? A man who only wanted other men, he was gay. I couldn't be that. I loved women. Right?

Except, you felt something last night you've never experienced before.

Shut up.

I wasn't gay. End of fucking story. It was laughable. I actually felt laughter bubbling up in my stomach, tinted with a bit of hysteria as it were; nevertheless, I wasn't gay. I wasn't gay. Now, bisexual? No, probably not that either. God no. I wasn't into men, for fuck's sake! Roe was...Roe was different. Roe was my best friend. My partner. My housemate. My lifeline in many ways. I loved him.

I couldn't imagine putting on gay porn and getting off to it.

That thought made me so damn uncomfortable I could barely sit still.

"I'm so sorry, Mama."

Shut. The. Fuck. Up.

I scrubbed my hands roughly over my face and wanted to hit something.

"I need you to tell me that's what this was, Jake."

I let my hands fall again, and I frowned at him. That was the second time he'd said something like "I need to hear" and "I need you to tell me."

"You got scared," he repeated. "You don't wanna lose me—so you got hammered, and we went too far. That's all this was."

Was he trying to convince me or himself?

It dawned on me that last night was in the way for him. An obstacle. He had to settle our hookup, make sense of it, in order to move on to deal with Sandra and their journey toward parenthood.

I found myself in a spot where I didn't fucking know what had happened. But I did know what *wasn't* the case, and that was one of them. What he'd just said didn't ring true in my ears. I hadn't crossed the line because I'd been scared. I'd made a move because I'd wanted to get closer to him. I'd been so fucking drawn to him.

And I was scared shitless to think that might still be true. That, if he leaned in now, I might want to close the distance, even in a sober state.

I couldn't make heads or tails of any of my reactions. Moving closer, recoiling out of reflex, pushing, pulling away, being drawn in, hightailing it outta there.

In the end, I wasn't sure my truth mattered. This was about Roe. His head was fucked because he was overwhelmed with everything changing so suddenly, and my giving him an easy out would allow him to make a decision.

Considering I didn't exactly know what my truth was, putting him first was the only way to go.

"Yeah, I got scared," I replied quietly. "I don't wanna lose you."

A breath gusted out of him, and he reached forward and grabbed my hands. I clutched his instinctively, and a stream of warmth slithered through me for a couple seconds. That still felt so good. Being close to him.

"We're in this for life, bro," he murmured. "You'll never lose me."

I swallowed and nodded once. Roe was smiling, but it didn't reach his eyes.

Our friendship was, without a doubt, the most sacred thing I had outside of being Colin's father, and I was genuinely looking forward to seeing Roe join me on that path. But even with our friendship secure—even though last night didn't ruin anything for us—something was going to change.

"Is there anythin' about last night you wanna hash out?" I asked. I had to be a better friend. I'd made this all about me, almost. But if I wasn't mistaken, last night had been his first experience with a dude, and unlike me, that was part of his sexuality. "I didn't hurt you, did I?"

He flashed a quick little grin and squeezed my hands. "Nope. Last night was hot. But you don't gotta worry—I'm not pinin' or anything. You're just sexy as fuck, and I love you."

I grinned too. And I let out a laugh. That was the Roe I knew. Always so honest.

I gave him my standard line. "Same."

The sexy part included. I could be objective enough. Or whatever.

His eyes gleamed with amusement. "You were more vocal last night."

I always was when I was drunk.

I shook my head and withdrew my hands, and I leaned back to get comfortable again. This was the best solution. I'd given myself an easy out too. He could move on, we were solid, and I didn't have to think about what the fuck was going on with me.

"It'll be a minute before I get that drunk again," I chuckled. "That headache today was no joke."

More than that, I worried about myself. If anyone else told me they could only be honest after they'd had a few drinks, I would've said they had a drinking problem. A bit of liquid courage was one thing, but to be true to oneself? That deserved its spotlight in sobriety too.

"I don't get the hangover headaches to that degree. I throw up, and then I feel better. And I eat my body weight in takeout." He clapped his thighs and stood up. "On that note, pizza?"

"Finally."

"Wait up, Bear." I grabbed the boy before he could run out, and I made sure his sandals were strapped properly. "There you go."

He was going through an...interesting phase. He hated wearing clothes. If he got his way, he'd run around naked all day. As it was, Nikki and I insisted on a diaper, sandals, and a T-shirt when he was outside.

We returned to the front yard, and I gave Grandma a glass of sweet tea.

"Thank you, dear. Could you please move the umbrella a smidgen for me?"

"Yes, ma'am." I glanced up at the sun, then repositioned the umbrella so Grandma was under the shade.

She much preferred the front yard to the back. Swimming pools had never been her thing, though she did meet up with her girlfriends every morning for water aerobics for seniors at her community back in Florida.

Colin darted over to his blanket, where he resumed playing with his toys, and I went back to pruning the rosebushes. I'd already done the lemon tree, the avocado tree, and the potted herbs. Nikki was coming over later, and she never declined fresh herbs from the garden. It wasn't like Roe and I used them. I just liked to grow them.

"The figs are comin' along wonderfully, Jake," Grandma noted. "Have you harvested any?"

"Yeah, they're really good. Breakfast around here beats any hotel buffet, lemme tell you." I liked my yogurt in the morning, and in the summer, we had so much fresh fruit. I loved that.

Next year, I was hoping to add passion fruit and some more vegetables.

We ate a lot of produce, because it was easy. Anyone could chop vegetables for taco fixings or cut fruit for snacks. With both Roe and me somewhat challenged in the kitchen, more often than not, we threw something on the grill or ordered take-out. And when the overcooked pasta met its fate in the sink or the burned potatoes ended up in the compost, meat and vegetables were what remained.

Haley had given me a cookbook in sheer desperation. She couldn't understand how one failed at making pasta.

So far, I'd used the book to kill a spider. I generally let them outside, but black widows had no place on our property. Plus, Roe was deathly afraid.

Glancing over at Grandma, I smiled a little when I noticed she was dozing off. It felt good to have her here. She'd injured herself last year, and knee surgery had put a stop to a couple visits. But now she'd recovered, and she was here for two weeks this time. Two weeks of July heat.

Two weeks of the calm before the storm. Filming was about

to begin, and every company involved in *Travel Back* was in the final stages of preproduction. On July 17, we were off to Italy, then Slovenia and Poland. Mexico a few weeks later, and on it went.

Roe and I were ready for the madness. He would make a couple trips back home to take Sandra to the doctor's—and to be present—and I was flying Haley and Colin out to see me once or twice too. But right now, the only thing we had on our plate was recording a bunch of podcasts so we didn't lose our viewers and listeners.

"Dada, dis one?"

I looked over at Colin, finding him pointing at a weed in the flower bed next to the fig tree.

"Yeah, you can pull that one." I nodded. "Good job, baby. That's a weed. We don't want those."

He grinned widely and yanked it out.

Bringing him with me in the mornings when I picked a couple fruits and pruned mindlessly was leaving a mark. Colin knew that Daddy didn't like the teeny tiny plants growing in the ground. Except for the time I'd planted a succulent garden along the back of the pool and he'd run over to me with a whole aloe plant and a proud smile. It'd been a learning experience for both of us—and a source of entertainment for Roe.

Speaking of the devil...

Roe was here. I caught a flash of blue on the other side of the hedge, rolling up on the driveway, letting me know that Roe was keeping his latest impulse buy. A bright-blue sports car that just wasn't like my buddy.

I wouldn't go so far as to say he was going through a crisis, but the recent events sure had resulted in a few uncharacteristic reactions. Mid-April, when he'd agreed to live part-time at Sandra's place, he'd signed up for motorcycle lessons. I'd talked him out of it. A couple weeks ago, when Sandra came over for dinner and sported a diamond ring on her finger, Roe got a tattoo. Nothing Sandra-related, thank fuck. It was a dove descending from the sky, a tribute to his parents. And…just a couple days ago, after they'd set the wedding date, he'd come home with that dumb sports car.

To be honest, the whole fucking thing was surreal, and I didn't think the wedding was actually gonna take place. He may have moved some clothes over to Sandra's house, and his bedroom had been converted into a guest room, but he was almost always here. Morning, day, night.

I was keeping my cool.

Nikki and Haley freaked out enough as it was. They couldn't believe him. That he would marry someone he didn't love.

I wiped some sweat off my forehead as he walked through the gate, and Colin lit up at the sight of him.

"Unca Roe, hiii!" He was quick to get to his feet and run over.

I smiled.

So did Roe, and he picked Colin up. "Hey, my little champ. How are you?"

"Hi, hi, hi!" Colin beamed and smushed Roe's cheeks together. My boy always found that hilarious.

Grandma woke up in the commotion and grinned fondly at the exchange. "Good mornin', dearest."

"Mornin', Grandma JoJo." He went over to her and dipped down to kiss her cheek. "How the hell do you look more beautiful every time I see you?"

I snorted softly and tossed the shears into my bucket on the lawn.

"Don't you butter me up," she scolded good-naturedly. "I see you haven't returned that monstrosity of a car yet."

Tell 'im, Grams.

"I'm keeping it," he insisted. "It's good to have a getaway car."

I cocked a brow and walked closer. "Why, are you plannin' an escape?"

The runaway groom.

"Funny," he deadpanned. "You ready to work?"

I nodded with a dip of my chin. We'd timed it well with Colin's nap time. He was an early napper and got tired around eleven, so he'd be easy for Grandma to watch. Bedtime at night was a whole other shitshow, but that magic hour shortly before lunch was smooth sailing. He'd crawl up on the couch and fall asleep to cartoons.

I helped Grandma out of her chair and guided her into the living room, and I ensured she had everything she needed within reach. Her phone and crossword puzzle, the remote controls, sippy cup for Colin, sweet tea for Grandma. I also locked the patio doors and the front door while Roe put on Colin's favorite cartoon.

"You be a good boy for Nanny now, Colin." I dipped down and smooched his forehead. "Daddy and Uncle Roe will be back soon."

I still wasn't a fan of "Nanny," but it was what we had. Nana and Pop were Nikki's parents, and my own folks were the distant Grandma and Grandpa who occasionally popped up on Skype.

Colin grunted as he wrestled with his blanket.

"Let me help you, sugar." Grandma adjusted her glasses, then leaned over to tuck Colin in. He was a true cuddler, my boy. "You can go, Jake. This may surprise you, but I've done this before."

I grinned half sheepishly. Sure, she had. But not at the age of eighty-six. Just because she was sharp and active for her age didn't mean she could chase down a toddler.

My grandma was cool, though. She'd taken an iPhone class at her community center and drove around in a custom-painted golf cart she'd aptly named Pink, after the singer. She was Grandma's favorite, along with Cole Porter.

After reminding her to text me—or call—if she needed anything, I told her that Haley would be here with lunch in an hour or so, and then Roe and I excused ourselves to get some work done in the studio. Once we'd brought coffee, obviously. We couldn't possibly do a podcast without our marketing mugs. *Off Topic with Roe Finlay and Jake Denver* was printed on a lot of shit these days.

We knew the drill the second we set foot in the studio. I prepared the camera in the corner, and Roe got the laptop running and helped me with the sound equipment. Some viewers had complained about the sound once we'd made our podcasts available on YouTube as well, so we'd doubled up and went with a separate mic for the video footage. Not unlike the one I used when we filmed on location.

"By the way, we might wanna think about promoting Haley," Roe mentioned. "She's starting to get business inquiries through social."

"Oh yeah? What is it this time?" I got comfortable in my chair and put on my headphones.

I reckoned the next step up for my sister would be management. Lord knew she'd prepared for it. She never stopped studying. She could probably share that responsibility with Seth.

"A game show." Roe smirked and waggled his brows at me. "You ever hear of *Know Your BFF*?"

Uh. Vaguely. It rang a bell, maybe. Horrible title.

"Remind me," I requested. "Wait—isn't that on CBS?"

"Yeah, they were renewed for a final season," he replied. "Basically, you compete with your best friend, and they mix it up with both celebrities and regular people. They're wondering if we're interested. It's short notice because two of the original contestants had to bail, so we'd head up to Studio City next week."

Jesus. Roe and I weren't fucking celebrities. Possibly in LA and... I mean, we had our bubble online. Fame looked different these days. I'd grown up with the view of celebrities like A-list actors and those big names you saw on the red carpets, and that just wasn't how it worked anymore. In part, anyway. You could be a celebrity in a remote corner of the internet, make bank, sign autographs—all that—but out in the real world, so to speak, nobody had heard of you.

To appear on a big network like that seemed awfully official.

"Do you think this is exposure that would benefit us?" I asked hesitantly. Because in the end, that was my reason for saying yes to these hooplas. We'd done some minor shit before, which had garnered more attention and, most importantly, more connections. And connections led to more work. More opportunities.

"A whole lot, actually." He nodded.

I waved a hand in *there you go*. No use in turning it into a thing. My dislike for certain types of attention and being in the spotlight couldn't stand in the way of what I actually loved doing, and being out there, being visible, was what allowed us to keep going. Keep growing. A necessary evil.

Roe counted down on his fingers from three, two... "Good morning, you're Off Topic with Roe Finlay and Jake Denver. I'm Roe, and Jake is sweaty as fuck from a morning of gardening, so he's happy to give you the weather report."

I snorted a chuckle and reached for my mug. "Sure thing. It's sunny and hot in LA, and it probably won't rain. Back to you, Roe."

"See? Who needs a proper weatherman when you have us?" Roe said. "Does LA even need a weather forecast? It's one season all year-round—unlike in New York, where we have at least fourteen."

I shook my head in amusement and took a sip of my coffee.

"And if any of you out there bring up June Gloom in the comments, I'mma get real heated. It ain't a season." Roe really cranked up the Brooklyn guy on that one. "In other news, we have some questions from listeners and viewers. You wanna take the first one, Jake?"

"Hit me with it." I'd lost my dislike for this part long ago. Because Haley vetted all the questions.

"I guess this is because we mention Jake's gardening hobby quite a bit this time of year," Roe went on, reading from the laptop. "Macy from Tallahassee wants to know where you got the passion from and—let's see, your favorite plant to grow and your least favorite."

I was gonna have to tell Grandma to listen to this episode once we aired it. She loved this topic.

"It's all my grandparents on my dad's side," I answered. "Growin' up, we'd drive down to their place in Florida every summer, and I would help them in the garden. Roses were a favorite back then, and I still have a soft spot for hybrid tea roses. But these days, I think I prefer to grow things I can eat when Roe screws up dinner."

"Hey!" Roe straightened up and got defensive. "Who turned rice into pudding last week, huh? Sure as hell wasn't me."

"That's neither here nor there," I answered smoothly. "Thanks to my growing tomatoes in the backyard, we had something else to throw on the grill with the steaks, and you fuckin' loved it."

"Whatever—I actually know the answer to your least favorite thing to grow, because you're always bitching about it." He was good at steering us back to the topic, despite the title of the show. "Lemme tell you, everyone. The day Jake discovered that one of our neighbors was growing mint, he completely flipped his lid and ranted like a madman."

"Because you'll never get rid of it!" I argued. "Fine if you wanna keep a small pot or something, but in the damn ground? My God."

Roe laughed at me. "Jake is very invested."

"If you call me meme-material one more time, I'll gloom the fuck outta your June," I told him.

He cracked up harder.

It was always good to hear him laugh, I couldn't lie. These past few months had been a lot for him. The fact that he was gonna be a dad made him soar, and he loved his job, which kept him in high spirits, but the rest had to weigh on him a bit. Deep down, he had to question his own decisions. Right? Or was I projecting? Was it wishful thinking?

Perhaps I was the one fooling myself. Maybe he wanted to get married. I bet it was common for grooms not to be particularly involved in the wedding planning. Roe's only demand was the location. They were getting married in upstate New York so his family could all attend without traveling too far.

Roe eventually brought us back, and we moved on to the next viewer question.

I sipped my coffee.

"Xander from San Diego says he's hoping to become a film-maker one day," he said. "He wonders if there was a defining moment for us when we felt we made it—like, this is it, we're doing it, we have our dream job. And...he attached this meme that's popular right now—"

"You and your goddamn memes," I groaned. Roe loved memes. He loved to spam my phone with them.

"Hey, blame poor Xander! I'm just the messenger."

Yeah, whatever. I made a quick note to edit said meme into the footage later.

"Anyway, it's four words every woman wants to hear," Roe explained. "But it's been changed to so many things—four words every soldier wants to hear, every man, every car mechanic, autism mom, and so on. So Xander wants us to go with four words every documentary filmmaker wants to hear."

I squinted at nothing and scratched my chin, and the funniest response I could come up with kinda just popped into my head.

"We got the sponsorship," I said.

"Right?!" Roe laughed hard. "Oh man, forget about 'the award goes to' and 'we have been green-lit,' it's all about the sponsors." He was down to chuckles and smiled at me. "I guess that was a defining moment for us—when *Nomads* got renewed and became a bigger production."

Abso-fucking-lutely. I nodded in agreement. "Being able to afford the equipment we needed without renting it brought us a lot of freedom. Setting foot inside your house that you own—just you and the bank."

Roe grinned. "Don't get me started—fucking childcare? I was *shell-shocked* last week when I found out Sandra's already looking at preschools. I was like, our kid's not even born yet? But apparently that's a thing. The waiting lists are almost as outrageous as the price tag."

All right, talk about going off topic on a subject I wasn't a fan of, but that was my jealousy talking. If I could even call it that. I just didn't like Sandra. That was all. But I did like hearing Roe talking about his future kid, and the preschool thing was definitely a reality check for new parents.

"For those of you who didn't tune in the last two episodes, Roe and his fiancée are expecting their first kid," I elaborated. "Nikki's all over that. We went to some interview when Bear was barely a year old—so we're sitting there with a whiny baby in our arms, and a lady's talking to us about creative opportunities and developmental learning curves." I shook my head. "When I was little, Ma just dropped me off with a neighbor and let me run wild. And I turned out fine."

"I can *hear* Nikki objecting," Roe replied.

I laughed. Fuck off.

Filmed before a live studio audience…

How many times had I heard those words?

This was wild. A whole other world compared to what I was used to. The studio was huge, and a bunch of people were running around to prepare for the next shoot. Roe and I had fucking makeup on, thankfully the subtle kind that just gave you a better complexion.

Two box-shaped booths dominated the center of the stage; that was where the two competing teams would sit. Where Roe and I would sit. And the other "BFF" couple, two guys from San Francisco who'd gained fame for an animated series on Netflix.

Thank fuck we had both Seth and Haley here. If I'd known beforehand how major productions worked, I probably would've hidden under the bed. The legalese alone had almost put me to sleep. In times like that, I felt dumb and brand-new. I wanted to say any contract longer than four pages was excessive. But I didn't do that. I just wasn't involved in the legal aspect of things. That was for Seth to understand. He just told me where to sign my name.

We'd been quizzed a lot too. As part of the game. The questions centered around my friendship with Roe, so they had to be altered before every episode depending on the contestants.

They had the fancy sound equipment here, though. I could

appreciate that. I was a little starstruck, to be frank. The three cameras that lined the stage, propped on dolly tracks—they were worth more than Roe's ugly new car.

I adjusted the bodypack attached to my belt as some guy clipped a tiny microphone to my T-shirt. We were backstage, so I could only hear the audience on the other side. They would be here all day, because they were taping three episodes.

We'd been told it would take approximately two hours to record a thirty-seven-minute episode, and Roe and I weren't allowed to see each other until we were headed for our booth. For chrissakes, I'd been escorted to craft services earlier. They took this shit seriously. All so that Roe and I couldn't compare notes and prepare each other.

Haley stuck close to me and parroted every instruction I was given. It was okay. I needed the reminders. Who fucking knew being a contestant on a game show would be so dizzying? But at least there wasn't much of a script, aside from the structure and order of the show. I'd expected more to be fake. I mean, I'd read stories about others who'd been on these kinds of shows, and it was difficult to know what to expect. Some were insanely scripted and involved countless reshoots to get a reaction right.

The people around here had only encouraged us to elaborate on our answers and "be energetic."

Me. Energetic?

Product placement played its part too, obviously. My ball cap was brand-new, as were my black tee and my construction boots. My jeans were my own, thank God.

"Five minutes!" someone yelled.

The host, Bailey Carver, entertained the audience, and a buzz rushed through everyone backstage. That was when I spotted Roe for the first time in over three hours. We exchanged a quick grin and a chin-nod, and soon we were joined by Ezra and Tyler, whom we'd compete against.

Was it fucked up for me to hope we didn't win? Winning meant coming back in a few weeks, and I'd rather not hop on a plane in Slovenia, go all the way to LA, tape another episode, then go back to Europe. Or wherever we would be at that point.

"Remember," Haley told me, "you guys are doing the Hot Seat first, starting with you, Jake."

I nodded in understanding and felt a little nervous. The Hot Seat would be...interesting. When it aired, that segment would take place somewhere in the middle of the episode, but everything was out of order for the taping.

"Get the contestants to their marks!" a woman hollered onstage.

Fucking hell. This was what my life had come to? I wondered how I would react if someone had told me, when I was freezing my ass off in a mountain pass in Afghanistan, that I'd be here today.

On that note, I hoped not a lot of questions Roe got about me centered around my years in the service. I wouldn't call myself tight-lipped about that time, but I just assumed nobody cared. It wasn't a topic that made me ramble.

Roe and I were ushered onto the stage, where the floor gleamed blue under the bright spotlights. *Hot* spotlights, I should add. And in the meantime, an actual audience coach got the people excited and gestured for more noise.

"This is nuts." Roe spoke under his breath before we parted ways. He stepped into the booth, and I was ushered to a chair positioned in front of the booths, where I would face the audience and a rapid series of questions.

Bailey came over and chitchatted, but I couldn't be as talkative with all those fucking instructions running through my head. I rolled my shoulders and took a couple deep breaths, and I was reminded once again about the rules of the segment. Just answer quickly. It was sixty seconds of questions about Roe, one point for each correct answer.

Not to be *that* guy, but I wouldn't use this bit as a warm-up. It was like rushing into the most heated part of a competition right off the bat.

All right. Questions about Roe. I could do this. And fuck it, we should aim to win. While non-famous people competed for prize money, the so-called celebrities competed for donations to their selected charities, and Roe and I had our two go-to projects. The recovery project for California condors and a North Carolina-based foundation that helped war veterans get back on their feet.

Bailey returned to his mark, and seconds later, the taping began. I had to pretend I was already halfway into the show and sufficiently comfortable. Being good on-camera was what brought entertainment, so I had to lose the stiffness stat.

"We are back!" Bailey announced, holding his flash cards. "We have Jake in the Hot Seat, and he's about to prove how much he knows about his BFF, Roe. Are you ready, Jake?"

"Not one bit, but let's go." I rolled my shoulders again and accepted a pinch of relief at the laughter I received. Everybody loved comedy. Comedy was a great place to hide.

"That's the spirit," Bailey chuckled. "Sixty seconds on the timer!"

Fuck me. The spotlights truly weren't a friend of mine.

Deep breaths.

At least we knew the first three questions, because they were the same for every episode—and the only thing we could prepare beforehand. They called it warm-up.

"What is Roe's favorite color?"

"He doesn't have one," I replied.

That earned me a faint *ding* for one point scored.

"The first CD he ever bought?"

"D'Angelo, *Brown Sugar*," I said.

"Does he play any instruments?"

"My nerves," I answered. "But no."

Bailey chuckled. "His first vacation destination."

Fuck. Fuck, oh, it had to be his grandparents' place. They went there over the summers. "Uh, Chesapeake Bay, I think."

"How does he like his coffee?"

"Um—" Shit. I scratched my forehead, remembering seeing more than one kind. "Oh, right—it depends. Black when he's tired, otherwise with milk—oh, and decaf after six."

Ding!

Holy hell, I hadn't anticipated my heart pounding like this.

"How many siblings does Roe have?"

"Two biological, plus five cousins he grew up with and refers to as his brothers."

So far, a ding after every question. I fucking got this.

"What is the one thing Roe is terrified of?"

"Wait, what? He's afraid of a lot of things. But I guess spiders top the list."

I even heard Roe's groaned laughter from inside the booth at that one. Sorry for throwing you under the bus, buddy.

"What country is Roe's favorite food from?"

"Mexico." Zero doubt.

"What's his dream destination for a nature documentary?"

Aw, I had to smile there. "Patagonia." We'd get there one day. Norway was our close second.

"What was Roe's first job?"

"Afternoon shift at a bodega," I replied.

"In the early 1900s, Roe's ancestors came to America from which country?"

"Scotland."

"Where in New York did Roe grow up?"

"Bay Ridge, Brooklyn."

"Has Roe ever been involved in sports? If so, which ones?"

"Nothing organized, but he played a lot of basketball and baseball with his friends."

"When did—" The buzzer cut Bailey off, and the audience applauded. "That's sixty seconds! Talk about impressive—Jake got a full score! You can return to your booth, and we will be right back after this!"

Jesus Christ. I blew out a breath and rose from the chair.

Roe was on his way out of the booth when I got there, and we bumped fists.

"You killed it, man. I'm feeling the pressure."

"Good luck. If you fail once or twice, I won't be sorry." That clearly meant I was the better friend.

Roe laughed and headed for the Hot Seat.

I stepped into the booth and got comfortable farthest in. It was a little warmer in here, but the fan above my head should offer some relief. I took a swig of my water and eyed the tools we had to work with. Two notepads, pens, and two small white-boards. We'd completed a test round earlier, so I knew what kinds of puzzles and questions we could anticipate. The topics varied greatly, from geography and entertainment to science and math, with friendship-focused challenges added to go with the theme.

Yesterday, Roe and I had watched two older episodes too. There'd been a cook-off at one point, so they definitely knew how to mix it up on the show.

As everyone got ready for Roe's round in the Hot Seat, I rested my forearms on the desk and willed myself to relax. The hardest part was over, I hoped.

"Welcome back to *Know Your BFF!*" Bailey announced. "It's Roe's turn in the Hot Seat, and his buddy Jake sure set the bar high with a top score. Are you ready, Roe?"

"Absolutely," Roe said. He sat forward a bit and gripped the sides of the chair. With his back to me, I couldn't read his expression, but I knew what a concentrated and determined Roe Finlay looked like.

"Sixty seconds on the timer!" Bailey requested. "What is Jake's favorite color?"

"It varies, but he's a sucker for green," Roe answered.

Correct.

"What was the first CD he bought?"

"*Get a Grip* by Aerosmith."

"Does he play any instruments?"

"Guitar and piano, allegedly."

I smirked.

"What was his nickname in the Marines?" Bailey asked.

Oh shit. Would Roe rememb—

"The Cameraman—well, it became that in the last two years of his service," Roe said.

Damn, I was impressed.

"What year did Jake get his first camera?"

"Oh, I know this. He, uh..." He snapped his fingers, presumably racking his brain. "He was nine or—no, yes, nine. Uh, 1992."

Ding!

"Has Jake ever been involved in sports? If so, which ones?"

"Football—didn't last long," Roe responded quickly.

"Briefly describe Jake's first published work."

"It was a single photo—a journalist from the BBC picked it up, a picture of a Marine carrying a child to safety."

"How does Jake take his coffee?"

"Black like his soul."

I laughed.

Bailey chuckled. "Where's Jake's favorite food from?"

My amusement morphed into curiosity, and I pinched my lips together.

"Aw man, he's more nuanced than me. He loves island food and Mexican. Mexico and, uh...gah. Wait! Puerto Rico! That's it! Mexico and Puerto Rico."

Nailed it.

"Has Jake ever dropped out of college?"

"Uhh..."

Come on, buddy.

Roe scratched the side of his head. "I, no...no. No. He doesn't have a full degree, but he's taken classes, and no, he did not drop out."

"How many baseball caps does he own?" Bailey asked.

"Two million—no, I'm kidding. Crap. Uh, maybe thirty?"

Close, but twenty-six.

"Does he collect anything else?"

"Yeah," Roe laughed. "He saves napkins from local diners when we're off shooting *Nomads*."

I smiled faintly and rubbed the back of my neck.

"Where in Florida does Jake's grandmother live?"

"Outside Fort Myers."

The buzzer went off the second the last word had left Roe's mouth, and I let out a sigh of relief. He'd done well. Nobody could blame him for not knowing how many ball caps I had. Christ.

"Amazingly done!" Bailey exclaimed as the audience clapped. "Twelve points for Roe in the Hot Seat—you only missed one! We'll be back soon!"

No retakes so far. I considered that a win.

While the camera crew repositioned themselves for the next shoot, Roe rejoined me in the booth, and for the upcoming bit, we could chill. Ezra and Tyler were up for the same segment, during which Roe and I wouldn't hear a thing. A static noise flooded the booth as soon as Roe was seated, and our mics were muted.

"I guess we know each other fairly well," I said.

"Dude, I'm gonna get so much shit when we get home," he groaned through a chuckle.

"What do you mean?" We had nothing special planned, did we? Just dinner. Grandma wanted Italian from a place in Venice we'd introduced her to last time, and Sandra and Haley were coming over too. But with Grandma going home the day after tomorrow and Roe and me busy with the podcasts, it was gonna be low-key and over pretty quickly.

Roe shook his head and ran a hand through his hair. "Sandra likes this show. She told me if we score high, she might get jealous because she feels she doesn't know me as well as you do."

"Oh, come on. We've known each other for a few years. She entered your life two seconds ago."

He shrugged. "It is what it is."

Maybe it was mutual, then. Maybe Sandra didn't like me either.

I was cool with that.

"You know what?" He smacked my arm as an idea struck. "We're not gonna tell her. We're bound by that nondisclosure thing until the episode airs, right?"

He was reaching, but so be it. If he wanted to stall for time, we could do that. I was pretty sure game show contestants in the past had at least told their spouses how things had turned out.

Reality would bite him in the ass soon enough.

Later that summer, Roe and I got bitten by another kind of reality too. Our work wasn't all sunshine and roses anymore. We had so much to film, so many angles to capture, so many places to visit, that it took a serious toll on us.

Gone was the freedom we had in *Nomads*, when it was just Roe and me and our equipment—and occasionally an extra cameraman or two.

Travel Back was bigger. In order for the animators and graphic artists to recreate history on-screen, we traveled with a twelve-person crew that included a topography team and four cameramen. I'd obviously picked up on where this was headed in preproduction, but to be here now, I just...I didn't know, I missed the old days. Roe and I acted more like directors than anything else, and the only people we liked to direct were each other.

"More floodlight, Jensen," Roe requested.

It was the first time I saw a more introverted side to Roe. He'd never been the kind of man to wanna withdraw from people before. Ever. But we couldn't do that. We had to lead. It was still our project.

Several miles into the ancient cave system in Slovenia, we huddled in front of a screen as Shane and Martina worked on the wide angles for this part of the cave. We were far away from tourist groups and outside noise. Heat too. It was fucking cold down here. About fifty degrees, while it was a nice seventy-four topside.

"Make sure one camera drops to capture the river and the other lifts to get the ceiling," I instructed, keeping my gaze fixed on the screen. It was currently showing me Martina's view. She was goddamn amazing. Both Roe and I hoped to work with her again in the future.

"What do you wanna do about sound?" Roe asked quietly.

"We'll try to record what we can," I murmured. "If the original sound isn't good enough when we get to editing, we'll Foley it in."

He nodded.

I pointed at the screen as Martina angled her camera

lower toward the river. "We're gonna need inserts of the stalagmites and stalactites, preferably with the water dripping to showcase how the formations take shape over time." It was partly why these caves were so famous, because of the rock formations, the sharp spikes and columns along the ceiling and river floor.

Roe nodded again. "We'll do close-ups tomorrow."

Good plan. We had to call it a day soon anyway, to make room for the topography crew.

Roe and I didn't even like our hotel suite. Postojna, this part of Slovenia, was old and had so much history I wished I had time to explore. That was the whole point of my dream—to show what I was experiencing. Instead, I was living life through a screen, and our supermodern hotel was located a couple minutes away from the cave. Meaning, zero time to head into the town itself and stroll the cobblestone streets that'd seen so much.

Less than an hour later, Roe and I were on our own. We went up the elevator to our suite, and I threw my windbreaker onto my bed and kicked off my shoes. Then I went out on the balcony and took a deep breath. Nice view, at least. Rolling hills and mountains, everything covered in rich green.

The sun was dipping lower.

I rested my forearms on the railing and heard Roe come out too.

He came to a stop next to me. "I feel like a spoiled brat for complaining, but..."

I nodded with a dip of my chin, feeling exactly the same way. We were in this gorgeous country halfway around the world—*but*...we had no time to properly experience it.

"Once we wrap, I want us to sit down with Ortiz," I said. "Maybe we can do another project like Scandinavia. Miniseries or a special about a new region. Just you and me again."

"I'd like that." He turned a bit toward me and rested his cheek in his hand. "Can we talk about the wedding now?"

What wedding? There wasn't gonna be a damn wedding.

"What's there to talk about?" I side-eyed him.

He smirked ruefully. "You didn't even open your invitation, Jake."

Because it felt fucking unreal. They were squeezing in a lavish shotgun wedding when we were the busiest this year, all because Sandra didn't wanna get too big for her dress. For the record, they had a mid-October due date for the baby, but you could barely tell she was pregnant.

The planning happened so quickly—though, I could admit, it probably felt that way because I didn't go anywhere near it. Even so, the date had been set since July, and just a month later, we were approaching the big day too fast. Three weeks to go. We had another few days here, then Poland, then back to LA—for that damn game show—then New York. Then Mexico... And by then, Roe would supposedly be a married man.

Fuck it. I went with honesty for once. "It doesn't feel like you're gonna get married," I said. "You don't want a bachelor party, you don't have time for a honeymoon, you didn't even propose to Sandra properly—"

"We agreed." He cut in. "I told you. She and I sat down in Seattle and agreed that marriage was the best option."

"And you honestly believe that," I stated. "Do you love her?"

"I—I care for her a lot."

That wasn't what I asked.

I stared at him. Waiting him out. I didn't have to spell out the fucking obvious here. In the years I'd known Roe, I'd just... felt he was a romantic. He'd been so vocal about his dream of a big family, much like the one he came from. Love, happiness, children.

Roe deflated after a few seconds and turned toward the

expansive view again. "I think I can love her," he said quietly. "I think I *will*. Genuinely. I just—I have to work through some stuff up here first." He tapped his temple.

"What stuff?" I asked, getting frustrated.

"*Dumb* stuff," he retorted and rolled his eyes. "My brothers always accused me of being a silly dreamer. I guess they were right. I gotta manage my expectations a bit, that's all." He paused, making no sense whatsoever. "Did you know my aunt and uncle got married after a month of dating? They couldn't possibly have known what marriage was about, but they made it work. They raised five boys—took in me and my siblings too— and we're talking serious relationship goals. You've met them. You must've seen how my uncle still looks at my aunt."

I hadn't, but sure, I'd noticed they clearly loved each other. So what? Did he know how rare that was?

"Sandra and I make sense," Roe claimed firmly. "We both want a big family, and she accepts that my work will entail a lot of travel."

I couldn't believe what I was hearing. It was so fucking unlike him. He was supposed to shoot for the stars. I was the settler. I was the one who went along with "this is fine." Not him. Not my Roe.

I swallowed against the growing unease in my stomach, and I sort of lost my words. What could I say? He'd made up his mind. He was actually going through with this. He was gonna marry a woman I'd written off as soon as we'd been introduced. And now she was becoming a permanent fixture?

As Roe's *wife*.

Fuck.

A tightness spread across my chest, and I rubbed at it absently.

This was wrong.

So fucking wrong.

"I need you with me, though, Jake."

I flicked him a glance, and he inched closer to me. For a moment, I detected uncertainty in his eyes.

"I want you to give her a chance," he murmured. "For me. Because..." He broke eye contact and wet his bottom lip, and he hesitantly linked his arm with mine. "I guess—until the day I love her like she deserves, your opinion matters more to me, and I don't wanna get married without your support."

Kick me in the fucking gut, why don't you.

Sometimes I wondered if I was so drawn to Roe and his honesty because I was the opposite. I was the douchebag who suppressed my emotional baggage and denied parts of my identity. I was a coward. He wasn't. I was scared to unlock the box rattling with Vegas memories. He faced his fears head on and...

I lied to myself every single day. But if I dropped the act for one moment, at least to myself, I knew very well why I couldn't give Sandra a chance.

I still wanted to be closer to Roe than what was appropriate. Not necessarily the, uh...more intimate aspects...? Yeah, no. That shit freaked me out. All the while...it was always there. That urge, that need, to take one step closer. To take his hand and squeeze it, to hug him, to hold him, to fall asleep with his head on my shoulder.

He was good at invading my dreams sometimes too.

I was even better at suppressing them.

"Say something."

I cleared my throat. All right. I was already a pro at bullshit. If he wanted me to give her a chance, I could fake it. Just like I faked everything else. *Fucking coward.* This was no different from the day after Vegas. Giving Roe an out only meant I was giving myself an out too. Lying to him, *for* him, allowed me to keep pretending.

"You have my support. If you genuinely want me to give her a shot, I will."

He smiled unsurely and squeezed my arm.

If I'd been anybody else right now, he would've hugged me. That was just Roe. The hugger, the affectionate guy. But because I was me, aloof and generally uncomfortable, he didn't.

Except, now I really fucking needed it.

Silencing the warning bells that went off, I stood up straighter and hauled him in for a hug. He stiffened for a hot second before he exhaled a chuckle and hugged me back. Yeah, it was fucking tragic. How a simple hug from me could come as a shock.

I called it self-preservation. Maintaining a distance kept certain intrusive thoughts at bay too.

Goddammit.

I tightened my hold on him and prayed I wasn't too obvious when I buried my nose in his hair. He always smelled so damn good. Felt damn good too.

I closed my eyes and stole the moment.

"Is it Christmas?" he joked.

"Shut up." I rubbed his upper back and breathed him in as subtly as I possibly could. A guy still had to get air into his lungs, right? Yeah. "I'm still pissed you won't let me throw you a bachelor party."

Another lie. I was nothing but relieved.

He laughed softly and stroked my back. "You know what I don't need? To get plastered right before my wedding."

Why? We made such awesome choices when we were drunk.

Wait—was that a worry of his? No, it couldn't be. I'd been the one who'd calmed down with the drinking this summer. It actually felt better. Tipsy was nice. A good feeling. I didn't wanna get drunk off my ass anymore.

"I have an idea," he yawned. "Let's order room service and watch a movie we don't understand."

I smiled tiredly and gave him another solid squeeze. Best idea he'd had all day.

We ran into the next problem the morning after we'd arrived in Poland. Krakow, more accurately. Another town I would've loved to explore.

"What time is it?" Roe asked.

I checked my watch. "Almost noon. Gina should call within the hour."

Go fucking figure. Something was wrong with our permits, so we'd been delayed half a day. We couldn't enter the mine until everything was taken care of. In the meantime, we'd invited the topography crew to our hotel room to go over last-minute details. The table in our living room area was littered with documents, blueprints, and laptops.

"Well, if the weather clears up, we could get started with mapping out the topside area," Charlotte proposed. "We have the drone permit in order, right?"

I nodded. "Just remember the no-fly zone west of the perimeter. Mine property only."

"Got it." Charlotte turned to her guys and pulled her iPad out of her backpack.

I moved one of the laptops closer to me and zoomed in on the map of Europe. Rather, what Europe had looked like shortly after the continent had broken apart from Pangea and started drifting toward its current location. That was why we'd traveled to the famous salt mines of southern Poland.

Roe shifted closer to me on the couch and studied the map with a focused look on his face. "So it's this area right here." He pointed at the southern part of the country. "Or was it all of Poland?"

"I think it was more than that, but it got compressed over time, and then the ocean here dried out, leaving nothing but salt." I swiped to the former page where we had the illustration of Pangea breaking apart. "So when it was Pangea, where you have Poland—or future Poland—that was the sea. And nearby areas. It dried out, the continent drifted, we had earthquakes and volcano eruptions, we had the tectonic plates shifting, Africa crashing into Europe..."

"That's what pushed the limestone skyward," Roe murmured pensively. "The Alps, right?"

I inclined my head. "Did you read that book about dating the rock salt?"

"Not yet. It's on my list, but I've been so focused on the thirteenth hundreds."

Made sense. That was when they'd begun excavating, and the mines in the area became an industry. With Charlotte leading the way, Roe was gonna guide viewers through hundreds of years of the area's infrastructural changes. He'd studied for months.

I'd concentrated more on the past before the arrival of people. I had to know the history of how the salt had ended up where it was in order to know what to film.

Roe yawned and pulled out his phone. "We should order food. I have my Skype meeting with the geologist at Cambridge at three."

I side-eyed him, thinking he looked more tired than usual. "You okay?"

"Hmm? Yeah. I didn't sleep well, but otherwise, all good."

Food, then. Let's get some energy in him. I reached for the room service menu on the side table and opened it between us.

"Jake, we're heading out," Charlotte said. "Considering it's gonna rain most of the week, we might as well go for consistency."

Yeah, probably easier, too, than waiting for rare blue-sky glimpses. "Good luck out there. Touch base before you wrap up."

"Will do."

As they took off, I returned my gaze to the room service menu, but then Roe put a hand on my leg.

"Listen. What're the odds of us actually filming anything today?" he asked. "I can't reschedule my Skype meeting, and by the time we've sorted the permits, it's gonna be late afternoon."

I furrowed my brow. "What do you have in mind?"

He grinned slightly. "Let's head out. We're in a new ancient city—you wanna order another American hotel burger, or do you wanna find an alley pub with local food?"

I smiled. "Do you think they have Polish sausage here?"

That made him laugh, and we were suddenly way more energetic.

Five minutes later, we left our hotel in matching cargo shorts, an NYU hoodie for him, a USMC hoodie for me, and with my trusty camera bag. We didn't bother with umbrellas; the rain was letting up, and our walk wasn't too long.

I had a thing for cobblestone streets. They made me wanna take pictures of everything. From the gorgeous lampposts and the buildings to the shop signs and cars driving by.

Krakow was a beautiful city, with a painful past. Supposedly, it'd once been the capital of Poland. But today, I reckoned the city was internationally known more for its close proximity to Auschwitz.

We were in the middle of the historic center, appropriately named Old Town, so it wasn't difficult to find a place like the one Roe had envisioned. Instead of an alley pub, it was near the main square, and it had a cozy outdoor seating area with an extended awning that sheltered us from the drizzle.

We ordered beer and plenty of food, only some of which I knew what it was beforehand—I really wanted that sausage—and I let Roe's "let's see what happens" attitude be in charge.

I'd read about Polish beer and food being good. The time I'd met Roe's family in Brooklyn, he'd taken me to a bodega of some sort, where we're bought Polish pastries and pierogis. Fucking delicious.

"If every server's that good at English, I'm not gonna get to practice my awful Polish," Roe said.

I chuckled, remembering he'd practiced some touristy lines on the plane.

Since we both wanted the same view of the winding cobblestone path leading up the square, we'd sat down next to each other, so I kept my camera bag on my lap, and Roe nodded at it.

"Get a picture of that house wall."

I followed his gaze and immediately dug out my camera. Fucking hell. Despite the rain, the sun was poking through the clouds, shining a beacon on an old house wall still bearing bullet holes, presumably from the war.

"Good eye, darlin'." I peered through the viewfinder and adjusted the focus.

Perfect. Old windows too, with paint peeling off. God, I loved history on display.

When I stowed away the camera again, Roe was smiling, and it was nice to see. Soon I noticed the reason as well. The server was back with our beers.

"*Dziękuję*," Roe said.

The server smiled crookedly. "You are welcome."

Roe looked endearingly proud of himself and raised his beer my way. "Nailed it. Here's to Poland."

I smirked and clinked his glass with mine. "*Na zdrowie.*"

He gasped dramatically and put a hand to his heart. "You *learned*."

Well, he'd repeated the phrase a hundred times on the plane, so what choice did I have? Besides, he had the right idea to pick up some helpful terms and words. I didn't wanna be the American who expected everyone else to know English. As my old man said, that was too French.

Our food arrived shortly after, and it was the first moment during this trip I felt really fucking wonderful. Like I was the one experiencing what I wanted to show others again. I had to be that guy who took photos of the food too, fucking obviously. This one was for Haley and our Instagram. Plenty of sausage, pierogis, something called zapiekanka that looked like a grilled baguette stuffed with sausage, mushrooms, and topped with cheese and sauce... Oh, and fries for the table too. Because why not.

"I'm glad we went out." I gave his leg a squeeze.

"Me too." His best smiles were when they reached his eyes just like that. The dimples came out in full force.

Comfortable silence followed, because we went to fucking town on that food, and holy shit, it was fantastic. The only thing I wasn't the biggest fan of was their version of coleslaw, but they made up for it with the spicy sausage and probably the best sauerkraut I'd ever had. Roe and I were picky about that one.

When my phone buzzed in my pocket, I wiped my fingers on a napkin before I checked my messages. Incoming from Nikki.

> Sending hugs and kisses from your cranky son who swears he's not tired. And you're all set for your fitting with Antonino. xo

I grinned at the photo she'd attached. Colin looked to be screaming at the top of his lungs. Poor Nikki.

"Look at that." I showed Roe the screen.

"Aw," he chuckled. "What fitting?"

Oh, right. I pocketed my phone again. I'd respond to Nikki when I got back to the hotel. "Since this wedding is apparently happenin', I gotta get a tux. Nikki has connections—she set me up with some popular guy in Bel Air who's booked solid for months."

"Dude—you can't look better than me on my big day."

I snorted softly and reached for my beer. "Cute, but you're comin' with me. If you won't allow me to throw you a bachelor party, at least give me this. You said your tux fit weird anyway. Let him fix it. Then we'll do dinner and talk all night about our feelings."

I made him laugh. That's what mattered.

I loved that sound.

Another pierogi later, I was so full that I couldn't imagine the walk to the hotel, so I leaned back in my seat and rested my arm along the back of Roe's chair.

"Christ." I patted my stomach and resisted the urge to unbutton my shorts.

"Seriously." Roe puffed out a breath too, then hauled out his phone. "Let's do a selfie for social. I'm sure Haley won't struggle to come up with a fun food-coma caption." He leaned against me and angled the camera at us, and I placed my arm around his shoulders and mustered a lazy smirk.

How fucking fitting. I couldn't help but laugh when we inspected the photo together. He had ketchup on his cheek, and I had evidently spilled mustard on my hoodie. We were some pair.

I grabbed one of the napkins and wiped the yellow spot off my chest.

"It's all about making our followers laugh, right?" He

dropped his own napkin on one of the plates before he slouched back against me. "God, I'm so full."

"Mm." Me too. But I was incredibly content. Just sitting here with him, all that food, the beer, the summer rain splattering on the canvas above us—I wouldn't change a damn thing.

I rested my head against his and closed my eyes for a bit.

This was the life.

I guessed the only two people I would add to the equation were Colin and Roe's future ankle biter. It was so easy to envision us traveling together, the kids running around, us trying to show them places long before they were old enough to appreciate them.

Roe yawned. "What're you thinking about?"

Fuck, that made me yawn too. "Our kids. That we're gonna show them the world."

He hummed. "I can't wait."

Me either. "You sure you don't wanna tell me what y'all're havin'?"

Sandra didn't wanna know the sex beforehand, but Roe did, so he'd found out at their latest ultrasound right before we left for Europe.

He chuckled drowsily. "I'm a little surprised you haven't figured it out."

Excuse me? Was there a way for an outsider to even tell that?

I'd already asked once, and he'd just shaken his head and said I'd find out soon enough.

He nudged me. "Think about it. Between my parents, aunts, and uncles, we've produced twelve boys and exactly one girl. Sandra has three brothers. That's gotta mean *something* for the odds."

I inched away slightly and looked at him. "You're having a boy?"

They were having a boy. I could tell by the look in his eyes. He would've been just as excited about a girl, but that glint right there was confirmation of my guess.

"Keep it to yourself."

Goddamn, we had to celebrate. If only I weren't too full to move.

"This is fucking incredible," I murmured, unable to wipe the smile off my face. "Two boys in the condor family. They're gonna give us grays before we're forty."

His shoulders shook with silent laughter. "Condor family—I like that."

So did I.

Even though our project was sucking the fun out of filmmaking for Roe and me, I didn't wanna leave Europe. I wasn't ready. No matter how mentally exhausting things got, being out in the world with Roe was special to me. I missed my son something fierce—that was the only problem. Other than that...

Tomorrow was the day, though. We returned to the hotel after a long day of shooting, and we just threw our equipment on my bed. While I took a shower, Roe hauled out our bags, putting them on my bed too. Then it was his turn to shower, and I made a half-assed attempt at packing some of the stuff we didn't need until we got home. Most of our clothes, the souvenirs we'd bought. But then I stared at all the camera gear, and I gave up. We could do that in the morning.

After changing into a pair of boxer briefs, I parked my ass on the couch and turned on the TV. They had CNN and Sky News for the English speakers, and a riveting segment on a royal baby was more than welcome to put me to sleep.

I yawned and scratched my chest absently.

Roe came out with a towel around his hips as he was brushing his teeth, and I gave him a quick once-over. Nope, bad move. Too soon. I had too many undressed memories from Vegas. He was gonna have to put clothes on.

I swallowed and diverted my gaze back to the TV, and he rummaged through his bag for something.

Don't look.

We'd become a tad more touchy-feely since our talk on the balcony in Slovenia—not a lot, just enough for me to notice, and it was mostly coming from me. I wasn't maintaining the same distance. I liked to keep him close, rest my arm on the back of his chair, stroke his arm, shit like that. And that was bad. He had a fucked-up magnetic pull on me, so I wanted to blame him. It was his fault. But those moments were still on the safe side, despite that the itch I scratched appeared to spread.

No bueno. Less so if he walked around half naked.

"What're you looking for?" I had to ask.

He had his back to me, making it impossible for me not to get a peek of his ass. "The deodorant I picked up at the airport."

Well, fucking find it already.

I wasn't attracted to him, goddammit. The draw was intense but platonic. It had to be. I could even explain away the times he invaded my fantasies, because that was just those compulsive balcony thoughts all over again. The people you read about who couldn't go out on a balcony without wondering what it would be like to jump. I'd been so messed up by what'd happened between us; Vegas had left a scar, and now I had those compulsive thoughts. Perfectly logical.

And utter horseshit.

I clenched my jaw and forced myself to watch the TV.

The fuck was wrong with me? I wasn't gay. I wasn't bisexual. I was into women.

Roe eventually found what he was looking for, and I

managed to glue my stare to the screen as he changed into a pair of sweats and finished brushing his teeth.

I rubbed at my chest again, this time because of that uncomfortable tightness that sometimes flared up around my heart. I remembered the physical symptoms of anxiety from Afghanistan, though they'd been much worse. But they still bothered me. Having these hang-ups pissed me off. I talked the talk; I was so quick to be mindful and open and accepting... when in reality, I was anything but. I couldn't shake the shame I'd felt as a child. The panic and fear. The rambling apologies to my mother.

Occasionally, I ran out of energy to lie to myself. I could lie in bed at night, twisting and turning, unable to sleep, and think back on the feelings I'd had when I'd seen that photo of my grandfather and another man. The warmth, the...*rightness*, in a sense. An innocent introduction to something I hadn't known existed.

It was hard to put words to something I'd felt as a young child. The shame was much easier. Because Ma knew everything, right? And the way she'd reacted could mortify me to this day. I wasn't supposed to get warm and fuzzy at that shit. That meant something was wrong with me. I was gonna go to hell.

Over twenty years later, I was chasing the same warmth with Roe.

The way we'd been at each other in Vegas...

How fucking platonic.

"I'm so ready for bed." Roe came out from the bathroom again and yawned. "Did you set your alarm?"

"Yeah." We had to be out of here by nine.

He groaned at the sight of my bed. "Bro."

I glanced over at the mess of luggage and equipment. "I'll deal with it."

He rolled his eyes. "We both know you're gonna crash on the couch."

I didn't see the problem. It was a big, comfy couch.

Roe got huffy, and he yanked his duvet off his bed and came over to me. "I'm too tired to resist procrastination, but I'll help you later. What are we watching?"

He collapsed next to me and fanned out the duvet.

"A British royal gave birth to another British royal," I replied.

With his presence flowed a river of ease and contentment, and I had no problem whatsoever joining him in the procrastination. I lifted my arm automatically, and he stretched his legs out across the rest of the couch and leaned back against my side. Last but not least, I rested my arm down his front and planted my feet on the coffee table.

"Kate Middleton," Roe murmured. "My aunt goes googootz for all that. She and my mom legit mourned when Diana died."

I did recall a royal plate collection of some sort at their house. Just random plates on the wall in the hallway toward the kitchen, with castles and the faces of queens and princes and duchesses and whatnot.

"I think the only time my mother's mourned the loss of something was when her favorite housewife magazine became defunct," I said. "She wrote a strongly worded letter to the publishing house and everythin'."

Roe let out a laugh. "To quote you, bless her heart."

I grinned sleepily and yawned.

No fucking wonder Roe and I were killing it at that game show. At this rate, we might have a shot at going to the finals.

"We're gonna fall asleep here, aren't we?" He yawned too.

"Probably."

He'd get no complaints from me.

"Ladies and gentlemen, as we begin our initial descent, please return your seat backs and tray tables to their full upright and locked position and fasten your seat belts. Los Angelenos, welcome home. Those of you continuing your journey, we wish you a great day and hope to see you on our flights soon."

Goddamn, my *neck*. I groaned under my breath and rubbed the back of my neck, quickly noticing a sleeping New Yorker cuddled up against me.

"Darlin', wake up. We're almost home." I scrubbed a hand over my face and tried to shake the cobwebs of sleep. Then I grabbed my phone off the tray table so I could fold that up against the seat in front of me.

Roe let out a sound of complaint and pulled his blanket higher up. "I'm not ready."

I chuckled drowsily and rubbed his thigh. "I'm not carryin' you off the plane."

"Rude." He dragged himself up and pushed his sleep mask to his forehead.

The sight was just so fucking perfect. The blanket clinging to his shoulder, the sleep mask, his unfocused gaze, and the bed head.

I took a photo of him, at which he scowled.

That one was just for me.

When we landed ten minutes later, we sucked it up and went through the motions. Thank fuck we had Global Entry now, cutting the security process in half, minimum. But we still had to do two rounds of baggage claim, first to get everything that went with all the other luggage, and then the "special" line for all things oversized and overweight. By then, we'd met up with the rest of our crew, except for those who'd gotten on the Seattle flight in New York.

"Ortiz's assistant is outside," Roe yawned.

Good to know. Most of the equipment would be taken to Ortiz's studio. Roe and I were only bringing home what was ours, and that was plenty enough.

After confirming we'd meet up with our crew after the weekend, we parted ways again, and Roe and I pushed three luggage carts toward the exit.

Haley, Nikki, my boy—and Sandra, I guessed—were waiting at our house with dinner. Which I was really looking forward to. I hadn't seen Bear in almost three weeks.

Thankfully, we'd become pros at this part. Once outside, we helped James, Ortiz's guy, load up the truck before he was off. And Roe and I grabbed a cab.

I checked my phone on the way. More accurately, my schedule. Thursday today, just dinner and squeezing the heck out of my boy. Game show taping for our second episode tomorrow, then a dinner meeting with Seth and Haley. Spending the whole day on Saturday with Colin; I was taking him to the aquarium in Long Beach. Nothing on Sunday, tuxedo fitting on Monday... Then two days of work and producing more podcasts before we were off to New York.

Ugh.

Next Friday, Roe was getting married.

Eight days.

The four days we'd spend in New York, along with the game show, had been the reasons we'd ultimately decided against having Haley and Colin visit us in Europe. It just hadn't made sense, considering we were making an LA detour this week. But safe to say, any future trip longer than three weeks had to include a visit of some kind. I couldn't go that long without seeing my son again.

Now I'd at least get a couple weeks with him. My folks had offered to babysit while the rest of us went to the wedding, but fuck that for two reasons. I wasn't giving him up, and I sure as hell wasn't surrendering him for a whole week to my parents.

At the same time, I had to make some changes. Aside from what were now monthly Skype calls, Colin had only seen my parents in person one single time, and I was running out of excuses as to why I was keeping him from them. My mother was distraught, and my old man was annoyed.

Roe may not get a honeymoon before Mexico, but he'd be off work for a month beginning around mid-October when their boy was due. Perhaps I could convince Nikki to come with me to Norfolk. Ma would get to see Colin, and I'd have Nikki there as my emotional support human.

That was fucking it, though. My mother would have to meet me halfway too. If she wanted to see Colin more often, she could hop on a goddamn plane.

Sadly for her, her warning about California had been kinda true. She'd been so scared Los Angeles would change me. Boy, had it. Well...Los Angeles had made me realize a thing or two. I was no longer their somewhat obedient son who shut up and played nice to keep the peace. If Ma called me obstinate for not attending church with her, what would she call me if she knew I'd bartended at a gay club? Or...nope, leaving Vegas out of it. Fuck.

When we reached our street, I glanced over at Roe and shook his shoulder gently. He'd fallen asleep again.

"Yeah, I'm up," he mumbled.

I paid the fare, then got out to unload our bags.

The house was a sight for sore eyes, even with the hedge obstructing the view. A hedge that looked good because I'd been smart enough to have a gardening service here while we'd been away. I loved my sister, but I couldn't trust her with my garden. She could kill a cactus.

As Roe and I grabbed the last pieces of luggage, I heard voices from the other side of the hedge.

"Momma, nowww," Colin complained.

"I'm coming, sweetie. I'm coming."

I felt my face light the fuck up, and I abandoned the luggage and jogged over to the gate.

There he was. Fucking hell, he'd grown, hadn't he? To think he was turning three in a few months. He grinned widely upon seeing me, and then we were hurrying toward each other. The gate slammed shut behind me as I swooped him up.

"Home now, Dada!"

"Yeah, Daddy's home now, baby. God, it's so good to see you." I peppered his cute face with kisses, a little saddened to see the chubbiness fading slowly. But a little proud at the same time, 'cause he was looking more and more like me. Except for his coloring. He had his mama's beautiful eyes and a copper tint to his dark hair.

I had a thing for green eyes. Both Nikki and Roe had 'em.

Nikki came over with a beaming smile, and I pulled her in for a hug too. It was damn good to see her.

"Welcome home, you rogue."

I chuckled and kissed her temple. "Thanks."

Colin began rambling, something that was also changing. He was *speaking*. He picked up new words every day, but he was still my little bear who liked to growl and show me his mean face and claws. *Rawr*. Too damn cute.

In the commotion, I'd completely missed seeing Sandra, so it hit me when I looked back toward Roe. Like a sucker punch straight in the gut. She had her arms and legs wrapped around him, and he was smiling widely.

In that summer dress, her baby bump was more visible than it'd been a few weeks ago.

They really looked like a perfect couple. Sandra was all wavy blond hair and smiles, and Roe... Roe looked happy. They murmured to each other in between kisses, and I wanted to fucking hurl. A heavy, obsidian darkness descended over me, and I tensed up at the onslaught of jealousy. God-fucking-dammit. That hurt. That fucking *hurt*. I wanted to tear them apart.

Instead, I pressed another kiss to Colin's cheek and planned my escape. Get the luggage inside, focus on Colin, put on some music, hug my sister, eat, shower, whatever.

Cue applause.

"Welcome back to *Know Your BFF!* Our contestants tonight are truly proving not only how well they know each other but how badly they want to move to the next round. Jake and Roe received another *almost* perfect score in the Hot Seat, Jake with thirteen out of fifteen points, Roe with fourteen. But now we're moving on!" Bailey stepped between the two booths as one cameraman eased back on the dolly track to make room for another. "So we've learned through Roe that Jake listens to 'Zombie' by the Cranberries when he's in a bad mood, Zoey let us know that her BFF David can't sleep without his sound machine set on jungle noise, Jake had no problems listing all of Roe's Marine brothers, and David ratted Zoey out for her passion for famous quotes and proverbs. You know what this means! We have our next four topics."

Roe and I exchanged a smirk, and I adjusted my ball cap.

Game face on.

Bailey listed the topics, invisible to us as they would appear on the TV screens digitally. "'The '90s are Here to Stay,' 'Rainforest Versus Jungle and Such Differences,' 'The US Military Then and Now,' and 'Can I Quote You on That?' Here we go! Roe, are you feeling confident?"

"Of course," Roe replied, not missing a beat. "I'm banking on Jake knowing every plant in the rainforest and jungle because he's hella proud of our lemon tree at home."

I cracked up and shook my head.

Bailey was almost as amused, and he moved on to Zoey and David in the other booth. "What about you, David?"

"Not in the slightest," he answered smoothly. "I'm afraid any reference to jungles will put me to sleep."

He was funny. I liked him. He was a photographer too, so we'd exchanged numbers earlier. His job sounded interesting. He was essentially hired to document everything on a movie set.

"Well, Zoey, you're gonna have to make sure he stays alert," Bailey chuckled. Then he faced the camera briefly. "We won't keep you waiting. Here is the first set of questions." He turned to us once more, and Roe and I had our notepads ready. "The Cranberries released their hit 'Zombie' in 1994. List three bands that also had hits that reached the number one spot on a Billboard chart that year. Question number two, which is the second largest rainforest in the world? And on the US Military Then and Now—give us another term for *stand at ease*, and please explain what *ten-hut* means. Last but not least! Finish these sayings, quotes, or proverbs. 'Who dares, wins...', '*Gone with the Wind* in the morning...', 'Cut your coat according...', and 'Do not call the forest...'"

Jesus Christ. I scratched my eyebrow and scribbled as quickly as I could. Thank fuck it was Zoey and David's turn to go first this round.

Our sound was cut off as Bailey spoke to them.

"If we don't nail the military stuff, I'll never hear the end of it from Greer and Cullen," Roe muttered.

My mouth twitched. No need to worry. That was the easy one.

"Ten-hut calls for attention, and standing at ease is parade rest," I answered. "The *Gone with the Wind* quote—didn't we hear that in the filmmaking class?"

"That's where that was!" he exclaimed. "I couldn't fucking —yeah, that's the one. *Gone with the Wind* in the morning, *Dukes of Hazzard* after lunch. Hell. I'm writing that down. But the 'Who dares, wins' thing? I thought that was it."

I shook my head and jotted down the Congo as my only guess for the second largest rainforest. "No, it continues. The rest just isn't as punchy as the first bit. It's something like…" I squinted and scrubbed at my face, and I racked my brain. "Dammit. Uhh… Who plans, wins. Who suffers, wins—no, who sweats… Something like that."

"Well, you figure that out—I'll work on the songs."

All of a sudden, they cut for problems with the lighting, so we were instructed to write down all our answers within a minute and then take a ten-minute break. In other words, the break wouldn't give us more time to come up with answers. We'd simply go with what we'd written down once we taped again.

As Roe and I exited our booth, we were separated. He was ushered to one side of the stage, me to the other. Zoey requested a touch-up in makeup, and I didn't know where David went off to.

I let out a breath and grabbed a bottle of water from a nearby bar table. People rushed by, but it was otherwise empty and fairly dark in this area.

Roe had done well. He'd also guessed the Congo, so that

better be right. And he knew that weird coat proverb...? I'd never heard of it. He had solid guesses for the songs too.

I chugged some water and—

"Jake?"

I spun around and almost choked on my water. Fucking hell. Sandra. I'd almost forgotten she was here. As a "fan of the show," she'd tagged along as Roe's guest.

"Hey. Roe's on the other side," I said.

She smiled timidly and folded her arms over her chest. "That's okay. I wasn't exactly looking for him. Are you having fun?"

Really? Small talk? Now?

Roe's annoying plea reverberated through my skull.

Please give her a chance.

"Yeah, sure. Definitely." I bobbed my head, feeling a bit awkward. "It's more stressful than I anticipated."

She laughed softly. "Funny, it's exactly what I anticipated. I had a feeling I would see just how well you and Roe know each other."

Yeah, we fucking do.

Let me keep that. She was getting the rest of Roe soon enough.

I hated her, and I wasn't sure I'd ever hated anyone before. Maybe my grandmother on Ma's side. And Sandra made it worse by being so goddamn perfect. She was kind, spoiled Roe rotten with attention and affection, cooked like a chef, she was somewhat funny... Maybe she wasn't the sharpest tool in the shed, but she was by no means dumb. She worked at her dad's agency and apparently did a great job.

She cleared her throat. "I, um, I couldn't help but notice Roe still refers to your house as home."

What?

I looked at her quizzically.

"With the lemon tree." She gestured toward the stage. "It's probably nothing, but I can't help but wonder if he'll ever feel at home living with me."

Oh.

"I'm sure it's just a habit." I had no idea if that was true, though it sounded plausible. Roe was officially moving out after Mexico.

Sandra nodded slowly and glanced down at her belly. "The thing is, Jake, that...Roe can't say no to you. And...now that he and I are starting a family, I need him by my side."

I shifted my weight from one foot to the other and stood a little straighter. Definitely not liking what I was hearing. But what I liked even less was that I had no argument for what she said. Of-fucking-course she needed Roe by her side. That was where he belonged.

Not with me.

"Would it be super rude of me to ask for your help?" she wondered. "Like, if his excited work brain pushes forward to another project and then one more, maybe you can slow him down a little? Help him prioritize me?"

Fuck. Despite how much I wanted her out of my life, she reached inside me and tugged at my heartstrings with those words. She was pregnant and worried. She feared her own husband would neglect her because he and I had put work first for so long.

She didn't deserve to be mistreated.

I could reassure her with one thing, though. "Roe has dreamed of being a dad for as long as I've known him. That includes the whole family. He will put his family first."

She smiled a little again, more ruefully this time. "The problem is that you're part of his family."

Oh? That was the problem?

My guard went up, along with my eyebrows.

She seemed to realize what she'd just said, and she started backtracking. "I'm sorry—I didn't mean that's a *problem* per se, it's just..."

"Contestants back to their marks!" someone hollered.

Thank you.

"I'm sorry, Jake, I—"

"It's cool. I gotta get back." I left the water bottle on the table and returned to the stage, my heartstrings intact. Fuck her.

Remember to smile.

Be there for Roe.

Smile for him.

This is about him.

It's their big day.

I looked fucking dead.

For the life of me, I couldn't muster an ounce of happiness.

Albany, New York. Catholic church. Approximately a hundred guests. Everyone was thrilled for the couple about to be married. I'd greeted countless people I'd probably never see after today. Some, I definitely would. Roe's family wasn't just big. It was massive. Most of his cousins arrived with their own spouses and kiddos, then add distant relatives to that. And Sandra's family wasn't small either, though their guest list consisted of "important work associates" of her father's too.

I did my absolute best to shoulder my role as best man. I was at Roe's side from the moment he woke up till we got to the church. After we'd greeted the guests, his brothers requested a moment with him, so I stepped outside for some fresh air.

I could do this.

Smile.

Sandra's theme was Lady in Red, and I guessed I could admit I'd thought it was going to be tackier than it turned out. The pews were decorated with white and red roses. Roe's red accent was his tie. Mine was a pocket square. The maid of honor, Sandra's best friend, wore a red dress. Sandra's bouquet, red roses.

I blew out a breath and dropped my chin.

Get through the day.

I swallowed hard. All fucking day, I'd been assaulted by memories I shared with Roe.

"Okay, we'll totally edit this part out," he said, "but I sort of see us as condors."

I chuckled silently, watching him through the lens. "We're scavenging vultures?"

"Well, kind of!" he laughed. "Not just us, but LA people— especially those tryna make it in the business. We'll take whatever we can get our hands on."

I could see his point. And I could capture his lazy, dimpled grin as he scratched the side of his head and peered up at the hole in the tree. That was where he insisted a condor had laid an egg. He'd said it fit their behavior. Condors didn't build their own nests; they used what was out there.

"It's about more than scavenging, though," he continued thoughtfully. "Condors are survivors—with a little bit of help. Kinda like you and me. We get by, but not on our own. We have help too. Just like the condors around here had some thirty years ago when they were almost extinct."

I glanced up from my camera and listened to him.

He smirked after a moment of silence. "We may not have a ten-foot wingspan, but we're scrappy, aren't we?"

I'd read that condors mated for life too, which I'd informed him of when I'd been drunk off my ass.

Always a class act.

But the mating for life didn't include Roe and me, did it? Well, as friends. Nothing else.

"*All fantastic sights—and obviously we're not doing any of them,*" Roe chuckled, facing the camera once more. "*In this episode, Jake and I are hiking down a lesser-known canyon to spend the night in an actual ghost town.*"

"*The way you say actual makes me worried you think there will be actual ghosts,*" I told him.

"*No!*" he laughed and shoved at me. I smirked. "*But we have so many ghost towns in this country that've turned into tourist attractions—and this is one of those that hasn't. It's actually a ghost town. Completely abandoned.*"

Just friends and business partners. We had many adventures ahead of us. As friends and business partners.

I looked up as the sun poked through the clouds.

"*Anyway.*" Roe smirked at me. "*You're Off Topic with Roe Finlay and Jake Denver. I'm Roe, and Jake recently started a fun family tradition for us. As mentioned, we're absolute shit in the kitchen, so we tend to eat out a lot. And when we have Jake's son with us every other week, we wait with bated breath for Tuesdays and Thursdays when the street we live on fills up with food trucks.*"

A fun family tradition. I guessed we'd have less time for that now. When we came back from a shoot, he'd go home to his actual family. His wife and son. Maybe they would go to the food trucks together.

No, Sandra would have dinner ready, of course. She could cook.

They would start their own family traditions.

"*Thank you, by the way, for…you know. I feel better.*"

He didn't need me to elaborate. He glanced up at the Lights again. "*Don't get uncomfortable now, Jake, but I love you. You're my brother. I'm glad I was there. And I'm sorry you had to go through something like that growing up."*

He'd told me I could call whenever. Just a few weeks ago, when he'd said he was moving out after the wedding, he'd said I could call whenever, and it'd felt like a slap in the face. Me? Calling him? No, I wanted to spend every fucking minute with him. He was the guy I never called, because he was right next to me. He'd caught my panic in Norway. He'd been there for every drunken ramble. He'd made me open up. We'd nursed each other's flus and man colds.

"Can I get you anythin' else?" I asked.

"Yeah." He coughed into his fist and reached for his pizza. "Keep me company. We'll put on a movie or something."

We could do that. I excused myself to get the rest of the pizza from the kitchen—and a Coke—and I made a quick detour to my own room to change from my jeans into basketball shorts. I would just sit on the couch in the living room by myself otherwise, so this worked for me.

Roe made room for me on his bed and turned on the TV. "Have you decided what you wanna do for your thirtieth? I still vote for Vegas, you know."

Then there was Vegas.

Just friends?

I clenched my jaw and swallowed the emotions threatening to take over.

"Jake—there you are."

I looked over my shoulder and spotted Nikki coming out.

"Where's Colin?" I asked.

"Kidnapped by Roe's sister." She smiled and slipped her hand into mine.

I gave it a squeeze and managed to smile back, if only a little. "I'm sorry I didn't tell you before—you look beautiful."

Her gaze softened, and she sighed. "You look downright depressed, honey."

Shit. What little energy I had left just drained out of me, and I cursed myself to the fiery pits of hell for cracking. I blinked past the sudden sting in my eyes, and every mother-fucking fiber of me screamed for *help. Help me.* I couldn't do this anymore. I needed help. Thirty years of confusion, suppressed memories, overwhelming feelings, and denial had caught up with me.

"Talk to me, Jake," Nikki pleaded.

I sniffled and cleared my throat. Fuck, fuck, fuck. I couldn't lose it here. Not now. I had to hold it together until tonight, at least.

"I think—I think I need to talk to someone." I quickly brushed at my cheek when a tear rolled down. My chest seized up painfully, and I sniffled again. Oh God, not now. Not now. "A professional, I mean."

"Okay. Okay—I'll help you. We'll find you someone, okay? I'm with you, Jake."

When she snuck closer and hugged me, my last resolve almost shattered completely.

"You have my support. If you genuinely want me to give her a shot, I will."

He smiled unsurely and squeezed my arm.

If I'd been anybody else right now, he would've hugged me. That was just Roe. The hugger, the affectionate guy. But because I was me, aloof and generally uncomfortable, he didn't.

Except, now I really fucking needed it.

Silencing the warning bells that went off, I stood up straighter and hauled him in for a hug. He stiffened for a hot second before he exhaled a chuckle and hugged me back. Yeah, it was fucking tragic. How a simple hug from me could come as a shock.

I called it self-preservation. Maintaining a distance kept certain intrusive thoughts at bay too.

Goddammit.

I tightened my hold on him and prayed I wasn't too obvious when I buried my nose in his hair. He always smelled so damn good. Felt damn good too.

I closed my eyes and stole the moment.

Mortification flooded me when a pathetic whimper slipped out, and I squeezed Nikki to me and hoped she wouldn't say anything.

Fuck, everything hurt too much.

Sixty seconds. I allowed myself one minute. Then I would get my shit together and head back inside. The wedding was about to start. I had to be there for Roe.

"Oh, Jake. Sweetie—this has to be about Roe. It is, isn't it?" She reached up and brushed her thumbs under my eyes.

I exhaled shakily and nodded once, then stepped back and pressed the heels of my palms against my eyes. Holy fuck—a single nod, but it was the closest I'd come to admitting the truth. I just couldn't lie anymore. What was the point if I reacted this way to my best friend getting married? I had no bullshit to hide behind any longer. *Everything* was about Roe.

"I knew it," she said. "I'm gonna go get him. It's not too late—"

"Don't." I was quick to grab her arm, and I gave her a firm stare, probably laced with more desperation than anything else.

"I need you to tell me that's what this was, Jake."

I let my hands fall again, and I frowned at him. That was the second time he'd said something like "I need to hear" and "I need you to tell me."

"You got scared," he repeated. "You don't wanna lose me—so you got hammered, and we went too far. That's all this was."

Was he trying to convince me or himself?

It dawned on me that last night was in the way for him. An obstacle. He had to settle our hookup, make sense of it, in order to move on to deal with Sandra and their journey toward parenthood.

"It's his wedding day," I told Nikki. "We're not gonna do squat. I don't even know what that would be—or what I would say. That's why I need help. I'm a fucking shitshow."

She gave me a frustrated glare, but I wasn't backing down. If anything, I got my resolve stitched up again, and I managed to push down my emotions where they belonged.

"I'm supposed to be the stubborn one," she muttered irritably.

I felt my mouth twist. "We're leaving the happy couple alone. You can help me find a shrink when we get home."

She wasn't pleased, and hell, neither was I. But for the millionth time, today wasn't about me. I had two goddamn wedding rings in my pocket, and they were for Sandra and Roe to give to each other.

We made it back inside the church, and I had just enough time to sneak into a bathroom and splash some water on my face before I had to rejoin Roe.

The next time my eyes welled up, I was standing a few feet away as Roe and Sandra promised to cherish each other till death did them part.

Our lips met, and I cupped his face in my hands. A violent shiver tore down my spine, and I deepened the kiss right away.

He moaned as I swept my tongue into his mouth. He fell against me and kissed me back hard, passionately. Lust exploded inside me, and my chest expanded with a quick breath and the urge to take whatever I could.

He was mine tonight.

This was right.

I sniffled and thankfully faked it well enough this time. I

could smile, even though it fucking broke me. I could be confused about pretty much everything and still feel in my heart that Roe was supposed to be mine.

I loved him...and I still chose to forever hold my peace because I was so fucking lost that I didn't know what to do with myself.

Roe and Sandra were pronounced husband and wife, and after they kissed, he glanced over at me with a bright smile that caused the unshed tears in my eyes to roll down my cheeks.

"There you are! Fuck, I thought I lost you, man."

I furrowed my brow and glanced toward the man's voice—that belonged to someone I definitely didn't know. But he was coming toward my table, and he was staring right at me.

No, wait. I recognized him. He was in my class, wasn't he? Out here, I had developed a radar for East Coast people, and he had a New York accent. Otherwise, not much about him stood out. Average height, brown hair like mine, fairly fit, on the lanky side, probably a bit younger than me.

He sat down in front of me, out of breath, and removed his messenger bag. "Look, I'm just gonna come out and say it. I have two hundred bucks, I'm living in my truck, and..."

I swallowed hard, and Roe and Sandra turned toward their family and friends, ready to take their first steps as a married couple.

How tragically poetic. Roe and I had arrived at the church together. Now he'd leave in a limo with his wife.

We'd meet up with them outside the city. About half an hour north of here awaited a luxurious lodge-type of resort that'd hosted countless wedding receptions before. Surrounded by duck ponds, a forest, and two golf courses.

I was gonna give a practiced speech on how happy I was for the newlyweds.

I'd watch them dance to "Lady in Red" and cut their cake.

Fucking shoot me in the face.

"Darlin', wake up. We're almost home." I scrubbed a hand over my face and tried to shake the cobwebs of sleep. Then I grabbed my phone off the tray table so I could fold that up against the seat in front of me.

Roe let out a sound of complaint and pulled his blanket higher up. "I'm not ready."

I chuckled drowsily and rubbed his thigh. "I'm not carryin' you off the plane."

"Rude." He dragged himself up and pushed his sleep mask to his forehead.

The sight was just so fucking perfect. The blanket clinging to his shoulder, the sleep mask, his unfocused gaze, and the bed head.

I took a photo of him, at which he scowled.

That one was just for me.

EPILOGUE
2013

I wiped sweat off my forehead and tried to get my heart rate back to normal before I read the text Roe had sent.

> Ten fingers, ten toes. Meet Cas. I named him Casper after you. Wish you were here. See you when you get home.

I swallowed hard and looked at the photo of Roe holding his little baby boy, then tossed my phone onto my hoodie on the ground and applied more tape to my knuckles. The punching bag in my parents' garage had been the best feature of the house when I'd been a teenager too.

That was the case to this day.

Quick jabs, hooks, uppercuts, and crosses.

Two days, we'd been here, and I was already itching to fly home. Haley got it right. She'd stopped pretending. She never flew out to visit anymore. She'd had it with our folks. She'd broken free.

Why hadn't I? Because I was a sucker.

When I'd left Norfolk, I'd still made excuses for our parents' behavior. I'd found them to be fairly normal despite it all. The shit Ma spewed at times had been somewhat easy to filter out. I'd looked the other way, confident I'd separated myself from the more extreme views they had. Haley had shaken her head at me and said something like, "All right, if that's how you feel..."

Being here now, however...fuck, it was glaringly obvious I'd just been blind and ignorant.

I heaved a breath and delivered three rapid jabs, switched hands, two uppercuts, and then I eased back and gave the bag a high kick.

My muscles burned. Sweat poured. Anger fueled me.

"You really ought to at least teach Colin how to say grace, dear."

No, we weren't gonna fucking do that. Nikki and I preferred to let our son choose. If he wanted to explore religion one day, he could do that when he was old enough to make the decision himself. There'd be no indoctrination in my son's life. I didn't hate religion, and neither did Nikki, but we'd both been hurt by some of its practitioners. That was enough for us. I had my folks, and Nikki had once had a grandfather who'd used religion to control his family.

One could say we were touchy on the subject.

"You know, you and Nikki really do make a lovely couple. Why don't you give Colin a little brother or sister? Children are a blessing, son."

I grunted and panted. Jab, jab, cross. Jab, jab, cross.

"We're not together, Ma. I've told you a million times."

Nikki, though—fuck, I'd never loved her more. She took things in stride, and we'd grown a lot closer these last few weeks. In Mexico, I'd received daily phone calls and texts, her just checking in on me, giving a fuck, being sweet, and I'd made an effort to be more involved in her life too.

She brought some humor to my misery. A bit smug she'd been the first to figure out my attachment to Roe, she teased me sometimes about "forever holding my peace" being a religious rule I could break one day, and "Go on, confess your sins to the shrink."

I hadn't even gone yet, but I had my first appointment the day after we got back to LA.

I was nervous. I couldn't lie.

Putting words to my feelings wasn't exactly my forte.

I took a deep breath, which didn't help. The smells in this house... I'd suppressed those too. It smelled like my childhood. Food, oil, the vinegar Ma put in the cleaning spray or whatever it was.

On the flip side, my ma's intrusive prodding had actually opened up a conversation between Nikki and me. Maybe giving Colin a sibling wasn't a bad idea. I was warming up to it anyway.

Last night, when we'd taken Colin for a walk after dinner, she'd confessed that she had feelings for someone significantly older than her. The man was currently going through a nasty divorce, and nothing had happened. And she'd said, "If something ever does happen, I know he won't be interested in having kids. The two he has are in college."

"And you know...now that you're gay and all, there's always artificial insemination."

I flinched at that particular memory. Some jokes weren't as funny. She'd quickly realized that. But I guessed I needed to hear it. Just...hearing the word gay being associated with me. It couldn't hurt. I still felt a genuine draw to women—at least, I thought I did—so maybe...bisexual? God. I didn't know. Either way, the embarrassment and shame around those two terms had to fucking go. Otherwise, I'd never figure shit out.

I felt guilty as hell about that shame. Like I was insulting every gay or bisexual being out there, and that was the last thing I wanted. Even more so because Roe was one of those people, and he was the best person I knew.

I missed him so fucking much.

Backing away from the bag again, I lifted my tee and wiped my face.

At the same time, I heard the door open from the house, and Nikki stood there.

"Where's Bear?" I asked.

She smirked faintly and closed the door behind her. "He's watching the news with your dad. I think he'll live."

Okay. Good. And Ma was busy preparing dinner, so she wouldn't have time to stick her fingers into our boy's brain.

"Did Roe reach out yet?" she asked.

I nodded with a dip of my chin. "Ten fingers, ten toes. They named him Casper."

Nikki smiled and raised her eyebrows. "Why am I not surprised?"

For chrissakes. "Don't read into that. He's called me brother more times than I can count. It's nothing weird to name a kid after someone you view as a family member."

"Uh-*huh*. I bet he didn't view you as a brother in Vegas."

"Woman, I swear." I never should've told her that part. I'd known the second I did, it was gonna come back and bite me in the ass.

I reckoned I should consider myself lucky I hadn't given her any details, just that Roe and I had crossed a line or four when we'd been three sheets to the wind.

"Don't swear. Your ma might smack you with a bible," she teased.

I rumbled a chuckle and figured my workout was over. I wanted to shower before dinner. "Let's head in. Maybe we can tell my folks we're dressing up as demons for Halloween."

"Oh, they'd *love* that," she laughed.

I grinned.

*Jake and Roe's story continues in This Will Hurt II
It's time to get inside Roe's head.*

THIS WILL HURT
Part II

Excerpt

I frowned when I noticed the words Jake had scribbled on the notebook cover. Not on the dotted line in the white box in the center where you were supposed to, but in the upper corner where it was barely visible.

Therapy journal.

He went to *therapy*?

Without thinking twice, I flipped it open and read the first entry.

THIS WILL HURT II

Patricia thinks I should write down my feelings in a journal. What I feel is annoyed.

I grinned quickly, unsurely, fucking confused—was this happening? Jake? My Jake? In therapy? Where he had to use words? The entry was dated too. Christ, November 2013.

I shouldn't read another damn word. This was a violation of his privacy. I should close the notebook right fucking now.

MORE FROM
Cara

Cara freely admits she's addicted to revisiting the men and women who yammer in her head, and several of her characters cross over in other titles. If you enjoyed this book, you might like the following.

Noah
MM | Hollywood Romance | Hurt/Comfort | Age Difference | Standalone

In 48 hours, Noah lost everything. He walked in on his girlfriend with another man, and the next day a plane crash ripped his family away. Gone was the carefree man who'd lived his life in the fast lane of the film industry, leaving a forty-year-old shell that dwelled at the bottom of a bottle. But one person could relate—only one. Noah's sister's stepson who hadn't been on the plane. Julian showed up on Noah's doorstep one day, and it was a good day to start picking up the pieces of what was left of them.

If We Could Go Back
MM | Hurt/Comfort Romance | Family | First Time Experience | Standalone

My sister asked how I could stand the sight of my own reflection, but I didn't see myself in the mirror. I saw Kieran, the man who was only supposed to be my friend, standing behind me, pressing a kiss to my shoulder as he undid my belt. I saw everything I wanted that I couldn't have. Not unless I was prepared to hurt everyone around me. He was in a similar situation. Were we monsters or men?

Unshackled
Standalone | MM Mafia Romance | Best Friend's Father | Age Play | Hurt/Comfort

"I need a favor. I...I can't ask sober."

In the wake of the bloodiest war the our syndicate had seen in a long time, all I saw was him. Shannon O'Shea had lost more than most, and every fiber of my being screamed at me to pull him from the depths of his despair. As the father of my best friend, he'd been there for me when my parents kicked me out for being gay. Now it was my turn. I had to rescue him. But the shackles around my wrists tightened as old enemies slithered back out of the gutters, and my brothers-in-arms and I were once again on the warpath.

When Forever Ended
MM | Hurt/Comfort Romance | Depression | Second Chances | Family

At ten years old, Kelly and I were two rambunctious boys who carved our initials into a tree in the forest and promised to be best friends forever. At forty-three, it'd been twenty-four years since I'd last seen him—after I'd foolishly kissed him—and depression was threatening to suffocate me. Not even my wife and two children could lift the fog. I was riddled with guilt and self-hatred, and I knew I was slowly but surely fading away. Then one day, Kelly was back in town.

Check out Cara's entire collection at www.caradeewrites.com, and don't forget to sign up for her newsletter so you don't miss any new releases, updates on book signings, free outtakes, giveaways, and much more.

ABOUT Cara

I'm often awkwardly silent or, if the topic interests me, a chronic rambler. In other words, I can discuss writing forever and ever. Fiction, in particular. The love story—while a huge draw and constantly present—is secondary for me, because there's so much more to writing romance fiction than just making two (or more) people fall in love and have hot sex.

There's a world to build, characters to develop, interests to create, and a topic or two to research thoroughly.

Every book is a challenge for me, an opportunity to learn something new, and a puzzle to piece together. I want my characters to come to life, and the only way I know to do that is to give them substance—passions, history, goals, quirks, and strong opinions—and to let them evolve.

I want my men and women to be relatable. That means allowing room for everyday problems and, for lack of a better word, flaws. My characters will never be perfect.

Wait...this was supposed to be about me, not my writing.

I'm a writey person who loves to write. Always wanderlusting, twitterpating, kinking, cooking, baking, and geeking. There's time for hockey and family, too. But mostly, I just love to write.

~Cara.

Get social with Cara
www.caradeewrites.com
www.camassiacove.com
Facebook: @caradeewrites
Twitter: @caradeewrites
Instagram: @caradeewrites

Made in the USA
Thornton, CO
06/11/23 18:06:36

844bd237-2ad9-4fe0-9f5d-3cfdcb903888R03